Lovi

Joyce whispered. "... ethical—not if I ever want to finish and publish my study some day and be taken seriously. I think it would be better if we were...well, discreet about being lovers."

Neill didn't say anything, but his fingers threaded through her hair and idly wound the long, pale ends around and around. He was right next to her, and yet he was a million miles away. A year would not be enough time to know this man.

"You didn't hear a thing I said, did you?" she whispered.

"I'm a better poet than you even suspect, love," he murmured back unexpectedly. "I hear all the things you don't say."

Dear Reader:

SILHOUETTE DESIRE is an exciting new line of contemporary romances from Silhouette Books. During the past year, many Silhouette readers have written in telling us what other types of stories they'd like to read from Silhouette, and we've kept these comments and suggestions in mind in developing SILHOUETTE DESIRE.

DESIREs feature all of the elements you like to see in a romance, plus a more sensual, provocative story. So if you want to experience all the excitement, passion and joy of falling in love, then SILHOUETTE DESIRE is for you.

For more details write to:

Jane Nicholls
Silhouette Books
PO Box 236
Thornton Road
Croydon
Surrey CR9 3RU

ANN HURLEY
Year of the Poet

```
Nottinghamshire County Council


Leisure Services/Libraries
```

Silhouette Desire
Originally Published by Silhouette Books
division of
Harlequin Enterprises Ltd.

All the characters in this book have no existence outside the imagination of the Author, and have no relation whatsoever to anyone bearing the same name or names. They are not even distantly inspired by any individual known or unknown to the Author, and all the incidents are pure invention.

The text of this publication or any part thereof may not be reproduced or transmitted in any form or by any means, electronic or mechanical, including photocopying, recording, storage in an information retrieval system, or otherwise, without the written permission of the publisher.

This book is sold subject to the condition that it shall not, by way of trade or otherwise, be lent, resold, hired out or otherwise circulated without the prior consent of the publisher in any form of binding or cover other than that in which it is published and without a similar condition including this condition being imposed on the subsequent purchaser.

*First published in Great Britain 1986
by Silhouette Books, 15–16 Brook's Mews, London W1A 1DR*

© Ann Hurley 1985

Silhouette, Silhouette Desire and Colophon are Trade Marks of Harlequin Enterprises B.V.

ISBN 0 373 05233 2

22-0286

*Made and printed in Great Britain for
Mills & Boon Ltd by
Richard Clay (The Chaucer Press) Ltd,
Bungay, Suffolk*

ANN HURLEY
sprang from a family chock-full of lawyers, teachers and scientists. After a long stint teaching literature and creative writing, Ann realized that she wanted to *write* most of all. Although she has traveled extensively, she chose to settle in Albuquerque, New Mexico, where she frequently walks across the mesa west of the city for a glimpse of the Sandias and the majestic Rio Grande.

Other Silhouette Books by Ann Hurley

Silhouette Special Edition

Touch of Greatness
Hearts in Exile

Silhouette Desire

Chasing the Rainbow
Year of the Poet

*For further information about
Silhouette Books please write to:*

Jane Nicholls
Silhouette Books
PO Box 236
Thornton Road
Croydon
Surrey CR9 3RU

One

"Dr. Lanier, Lisa is in the waiting room."

"Thanks, Margaret," Joyce said hastily. Looking somewhat guilty, she closed the manila file folder in front of her. Only the initials, N.R., identified it but she locked it in her desk drawer before she left the office. Neill Riordan was not one of the young patients she saw regularly at the Bennett Clinic, and she did not want to risk her reputation as a clinical psychologist treating gifted children by slighting Lisa.

Lisa's mother exchanged a smile with her and complimented Joyce on her bright red wool suit. "This winter's been so bleak, it's great to see a spot of color...and appropriate for the season. You know, with Valentine's Day."

Joyce thanked the woman and nodded, slipping an arm around the silent, unsmiling child to claim her. If she looked like a promise of spring, Joyce was glad. Strong, clear colors were complimentary to her cool blond looks but more important, they were attractive and mood-elevating for young patients.

"Chicago is awful and depressing in the winter," announced Lisa as she and Joyce headed for their session. "I think we should all hibernate like bears."

Three short weeks ago, Joyce would have seconded the girl's sentiment but while Lisa recited statistics on cold and wind, she recalled her first meeting with Neill Riordan. The remnants of excitement and challenge drove out the memory of a sub-zero night. The visiting Irish poet was going to be at the University for only a year's teaching stint, but it would be plenty of time for her research into the development of a widely recognized adult genius.

If I can get him to cooperate, Joyce thought uncomfortably.

Neill had been charming to her after his reading of works-in-progress, but hardly cooperative. Julia, Joyce's younger sister and one of the "great man's" students and literary worshippers, had made the introduction. The next thing Joyce recalled was being led off by the big, brash, outspoken man to a local student hangout. She had explained what she wanted—his time, his background, his problems—while he explained poetry to her and his appetite to the waitress. And Joyce ended up paying for his meal. Famous poets, it seemed, often forgot the mundane details like bringing their wallets.

"I like the new science teacher, though," said Lisa as if it were a crime to like anyone. "He knows his subject and he doesn't treat us like kids. He's a mess, Dr. Lanier. I mean, to look at..."

"Tell me about him," Joyce encouraged. It was rare to hear Lisa approve of something or someone. "What does he look like? What are you doing in class?"

In the middle of Neill's reading in Weiboldt Hall, Joyce had leaned slightly toward her sister. "He's a mess, Julia," she had whispered. "Magnificent but a mess." Julia glared at her.

Her snap judgment, based on the man's overwhelmingly careless appearance, was all wrong; she had seen only the too-big tweed jacket in a nondescript color, the unshaven shadow on his square jaw and prominent chin, a wild brush of curly reddish-brown hair that needed taming and trimming. By the end of the evening, Joyce forgot her own uncharitable thought, and it didn't matter that his tie was skewed slightly to one side, the knot offset like a hangman's noose.

Neill Riordan was impressive and attractive without even trying. Julia and his other adoring graduate students thought he was a god—handsome, brilliant and exotic— but Joyce had realized it was an unpruned ease with himself reflected in his unstudied, broad-shouldered posture and a sense of untamed masculinity that surrounded him like an aura. When his gray eyes met her china-blue ones, Joyce had seen power and charisma there. What a career coup it would be to discover the roots and growth of that power!

"...So Mrs. Taylor and I made this bargain. If I go out to recess and *pretend* to play with the other kids, I get to do my own project with school equipment." Lisa wrinkled her nose in disgust. "It's dumb, but I'm doing it."

"A wise compromise," praised Joyce. "We have to give to get, sometimes." She pondered the wisdom of her own peculiar bargain. Neill had been willing to meet and talk with her, but only on his terms. No formal appointments, no office visits, no tape recorder or taking notes. The man could weave a soft web of words as easily as he could make them blaze with the fire of his poems. It was too haphazard and unscientific a schedule to suit Joyce, but it was all he offered.

"A green heart...how gross!" Lisa sneered with the average eight-year-old's expression of contempt. She got up and stepped closer to Joyce's cork bulletin board to examine the paper object of her derision in greater detail. She proceeded to explain with the average pre-med student's knowledge the facts about the human heart.

"It's a valentine. The color is the sender's joke," Joyce said evenly after the mini-lecture. "As a funny card, it's fine. It's not necessary to be anatomically correct if it's a valentine. By the way, did you make or buy cards for anyone?"

"No," the girl replied solemnly, "it seems silly."

"Next session we'll talk about the possible virtues of being silly," declared Joyce as she opened the door. She felt herself groaning inwardly. Just once, she's like to see Lisa do something silly and spontaneous.

Lisa looked at her psychologist with a mild horror. "Seriously?" The suggestion of a frivolous topic was obviously enough to bother her. But Joyce nodded and returned the conservative, perfectionist Lisa to her mother before the child could present another argument.

The emerald heart made Joyce smile involuntarily as she went back to her desk. She glanced up at it every time she paused while writing her case notes on Lisa. A thirty-five-year-old Irishman sent her something silly and she had done something spontaneous in return. She tried not to mix her personal life with her professional work, but the unexpected valentine had thrown her for a loop. She'd invited Neill to dinner before she'd thought about breaking one of her own rules. Hopefully, Joyce would have a chance to review her secret file of notes on him before he would arrive at her apartment that night.

He was reported to be a rebel with words, but he had been soft-spoken at their first meeting. Critics wrote that Neill Riordan was flamboyant and difficult and hot-tempered. Joyce kept remembering how funny and witty he had been at the bookstore he'd summoned her to last week while he was autographing copies of his volumes. He'd given her copies of *Harpstrings* and *An Old Woman, Dying*, teasing Joyce about wanting to pick his brain without having to pick up his books.

"You're not going to be easily pinned down and examined," Joyce said aloud, taking out her file on him. She looked quickly at the office door to make sure it was shut. What was she getting herself into? A psychologist talking to herself and not getting answers boded no good.

Tonight, Joyce thought decisively. Skimming her concise entries offered no deep insights on how to get Neill to open up and yield the material she needed. A dinner for two in a quiet, relaxed setting might give her better results. When she looked up and saw his Irish version of a valentine, a tingle of anticipation ran through her. It was so strong, Joyce put the file away and reminded herself she would have to be careful working with the man. She was a professional with clinical interests. Not personal.

"I'm late," Neill said without apology when she opened the door. "That's only one of my bad habits...one of the lesser ones."

He stepped into the tiled foyer and brushed ineffectually at his windblown hair with a large, squarish hand. With the other he gave Joyce a long thin object wrapped in red tissue paper.

"It doesn't matter," said Joyce. It was more important to put him at ease than to tell the truth. She filed away his lack of punctuality for future use. "The dinner's on simmer and we can have a drink or coffee, if you like."

Some people brought flowers or a bottle of wine. Joyce unwrapped the paper and slid out a silver penny whistle. It was such a strange offering, she smiled, and Neill laughed at her puzzled expression.

"The *feadog Stain* is not a child's toy," he explained. "You look like a musical woman and I'll be glad to give you a lesson."

"I can't sing a note," confessed Joyce. "I can't even play the tissue paper and comb."

She left his gift on the coffee table and went to the kitchen to check the stew. He followed her, filling the room with his presence and making Joyce very aware of his size. She was determined not to let herself be the topic of the conversation tonight or her talents or the lack of them.

"Is music one of your interests?" Joyce asked, dipping a wooden spoon into the pot for a taste. "Julia's mentioned how you bring many concepts from art and music into your seminars."

"I have a lot of interests," Neill said. He took the spoon from her hand without asking and finished the small amount Joyce left. He gave a nod of approval and dropped the spoon with a satisfied clunk back on the counter. "Good music, good food, good company."

"I wish you were more specific. One of the problems of my very brightest children is how often they get involved in one area and forget the rest of the world."

His look took in everything at once—Joyce, the room. She almost felt his open survey touch the length of her smooth golden hair and the column of her slender neck. She was beginning to wish she hadn't changed into such comfortable, casual clothes after work.

"I like to be part of everything the world has to offer," Neill replied slowly. "Traveling from place to place and teaching as I go helps me as a poet...and as a man."

At least they were talking about him. Joyce waved him onto her worn red velvet sofa and poured two glasses of beer. She sipped from her glass and congratulated herself on the plan. It was finally going well. Neill quickly described his last five years of wandering—Dublin, New York, Los Angeles and Chicago—and was reminiscing about how early he'd begun to travel. This was exactly the information Joyce needed about his childhood.

"I couldn't stay in one place too long," he declared. "There's too much to see, to do, and too many people to meet everywhere else. I'd run away to Galway to see the races or take off after a family of tinkers. My family called me their gypsy."

His revelation made her feel strangely hollow and it shouldn't have. Many geniuses were unsettled and restless people, anxious when their horizons were limited. Just because she was firmly rooted to one place, she couldn't let his nomadic life-style bother her.

"Do you get bored easily?" Joyce asked casually. "You know, need new scenes, new faces around you?"

He took a drink and she watched his throat move with the long, full draft. He wasn't quick to answer her inquiries. She made a mental note not to interrupt him again; every question only made him conscious of what she was doing.

"I'm rarely bored," Neill said flatly. His free hand rounded the curve of the sofa's arm, caressing the velvet and the wood. His gray eyes traveled just as slowly over her face, as if he were touching her. "There's always a surprise waiting for me."

"Like what?" She wished she had bitten her tongue. His look, piercing and eloquent, went right through her and gave her the answer before he spoke.

"You. I was vaguely amused when Julia trotted you up to meet me at the university. You were so sleek and modern, all business and right to the point, I thought. You caught me offguard."

This was not the direction she wanted the evening to take. He was getting personal, leading the talk back to her.

"I think we'd better eat," Joyce said. "The stew smells like it might be burning."

He stood up with her, ignoring her effort to change the subject. "When I saw this big, sterile, glass building, I wasn't going to come up here. I've met many women recently with hard edges and no heart or warmth. But once I saw this apartment, I saw *you* and it's a pleasant surprise."

He was surveying her lovingly collected antiques. Joyce kept silent while he took in the rag rugs, the odd furniture and the tin-fronted pie safe she had refinished.

"Why?" Joyce asked, regretting the single word. Why was she so uptight tonight? Relax, she cautioned herself. She could maneuver the conversation back to him, his interests, his life and not hers.

"There is something old-fashioned under your very crisp manner, your professional face." He sat down across the small drum table and smiled at her. "You don't want people to see the softer, gentler places in you."

There weren't any candles on the table and she hadn't cooked anything fancy because she didn't want to set a romantic mood. Still, a sense of intimacy surrounded them. Joyce concentrated on heaping the stew on his plate and moving him back to the right track, the one she had chosen.

"Writing, of course, puts many of your inner feelings on display, but you don't like to talk about yourself. Doesn't that seem like a contradiction?" She returned his smile innocently, confident she could handle his reluctance.

"Not *all* my feelings," Neill said. "Every man has his secrets and a dream or two he doesn't care to share on some local interview show."

She agreed, ladling more food onto his plate as he nodded at her silent offer. He had an extraordinary appetite for stew and life, it seemed. "I hope you understood that I'm not researching your background to be nosy, Neill. I can use insights to help some of my gifted children develop to their full potential and avoid some problems common to very bright people."

"And how will you help Neill Riordan with all this prying and probing? What's in it for me?"

Joyce looked up from her plate and discovered he was very serious. She swallowed her funny, tentative feeling along with the last of the stew. She wasn't used to being put on the spot or losing control of situations, but she wasn't used to dealing with strong, stubborn adults either.

"Well, you're not my patient," she began slowly, "so I can't offer you help with problems."

"No," he said in his low, thrilling voice.

"You probably don't want any more publicity, and my kind of study won't be widely read, anyway," Joyce mused aloud. She tried to ignore the mild prickle of tension between them, the electric sense Neill inspired in her whenever she was with him. It had to be because he was ideal for her study, she rationalized. She couldn't lose this perfect chance to further her work. There had to be a persuasive reason to offer him.

Neill laughed. "I didn't become a poet to become famous. I never expect to be widely read."

She glanced out her apartment window at the city's skyline, black against a navy and gold sky and already sparkling with tiny, numberless lights. "I suppose if we work together, you get some more of the truth about yourself—who and what you are."

His fork clattered down on his plate and Neill smiled as he reached across the table to take her hand.

"Beautiful but wrong," he said, bringing her fingers to his mouth and brushing them lightly with his lips. The pull of his grip was strong and it made the softness of his mouth more startling by contrast. "I knew you were beautiful the second I saw you at the reading, staring out of the audience at me. I knew you were wrong the minute you started in on all the wonderful results your project would reap. Truths about me, huh? I know more about myself than I care to; it's you I want to know about."

She kept her face composed and her voice level, but there was a throaty little catch in it. Neill was reputed to have a following of women who wouldn't know a poem from a pineapple. She wanted to make it clear that she was no literary "groupie." "That's easy. I'm a very good psychologist and an ordinary woman. My looks are largely due to the Lanier genes and my brains come from hard work and experience. If you give me back my hand, I'll get dessert and coffee."

He didn't release her. When Joyce started to stand up, he stood up with her so he could maintain his hold on her. His head brushed the leaded glass fixture over the table and set it swaying gently. Then he smiled faintly at her and let go of her captive fingers, reaching up to still the lamp.

"For all my size, I'm not usually so clumsy," he said. It wasn't clear whether he meant his conversational tack or rattling her Tiffany shade.

"No harm done, but I won't take any chances and have you clear the dishes," Joyce replied. She could still feel the warmth and strength of his fingers as she collected the old mismatched plates. Waving him in the direction of the living room, she was grateful for a few minutes alone in the narrow kitchen to collect her thoughts.

Ground rules. She needed to set them and get his agreement if they were going to work together. It was easier to be her usual objective and analytic self when he wasn't close, trying to charm and succeeding with no real effort. It didn't hurt to remind herself of pitfalls, either. He was sexy, dammit, and he knew it. She'd been warned by the lazy heat creeping into her hand and up her arm. He was dangerously appealing.

There was a muffled sound of delight from Neill and a soft wave of classical music followed. Neill evidently found that her cathedral-shaped radio really worked and was not just nostalgic decoration. When Joyce came in with coffee, he was studying it and humming happily along with the Mozart.

"We had one of these in the parlor when I was young." He straightened up, his face losing the reflected glow from the lighted dial band, and joined her on the couch. As if it were an afterthought, he unbuttoned the top button of his shirt and loosened his tie. "The Riordan mob would be spread out on the rug. Green. The rug was a vile dark green with immense pink and wine-red roses, covered with seven Riordans and my mother. When my dad was home, we'd listen to news, of course...."

She found she couldn't interrupt to lay down her rules. She had wanted his flood of reminiscences, and now he was offering them without prompting. His story made its own music as it joined the swirl of violins behind it. Joyce realized she wouldn't need to take notes. Neill told an anecdote as well as he wrote a poem, full of unforgettable detail and childhood joys and despairs.

When he stopped talking, Neill rested his head on the back of the sofa and peered at her from under half-closed eyes. "I see why you're good at your job. It's very easy when I look into your peaceful face and kind eyes to tell you about things half-forgotten. Do they teach you to look that way?"

His question broke the spell. She had not been listening as critically as she should, but had been sharing his feelings as intensely as if she had lived them. It was time to make her own rules and stick to them.

"No one taught me to look any special way." She tucked her legs up under her and cleared her throat nervously. "However, I was taught to set an atmosphere of trust. We won't accomplish much, Neill, if we don't trust each other. Talking honestly about yourself isn't the same thing as giving yourself away to another person. We need to meet regularly and alone. We need to be open."

"We're alone," he pointed out. "I didn't plan to share that last evening you came down to the university with your sister and her sullen boyfriend. They invited themselves along, if you remember."

She did. Julia and Frank spent the night sniping at each other and then Neill and Frank had argued the finer points of Irish history.

"Well, that's exactly what I mean," Joyce said, more confident of his agreement. "No more calling me up on the spur of the moment and arranging one of these meetings at some bookstore or student function."

"Not at the clinic," Neill warned. "I'm not stretching out on a couch alone."

"Dr. Kyler and the Bennett have nothing to do with my study," Joyce told him. "This is a personal project. I wouldn't dare use my time there or their facilities. And I don't use a couch."

"How about here?" He gave her one of his most disarming smiles. "I won't object to having a home-cooked meal on a regular basis."

"Then get married to a whiz with the microwave," chuckled Joyce. "I'm trying to make a professional arrangement with you, not set up dates. There's always your office, Riordan."

"And my house," he added with a distinctly sly look. "Or don't you trust me, Doctor?"

"We'll work it out," Joyce said weakly, "if you agree to a schedule of meetings. I don't make house calls."

"I'm very agreeable, you'll find." He shifted on the couch and moved very close to her.

Joyce became aware of his body heat and the faint scent of bay rum. She willed herself to sit still and resist the urge to retreat. She wouldn't discover much about the man if she was awed or cowed by him.

His eyes had widened, searching hers. Joyce studied the slight roughness of his chin, the hard line of his jaw and the fine seaming of lines at the ends of his compelling eyes.

"You haven't told me one thing," Neill said. "How much of me do you want to know? Just enough to explain me, Joyce? Do you want the poet only from the neck up?"

"I don't get involved with people I work with. There has to be some distance between us or I can't be objective."

His face came closer until she could feel the warmth of his breath across her cheek. His expression changed, became almost fierce. "Don't talk like a psychologist. Talk like a woman. I'm flesh as well as a mind. Does that interest you? Are you as curious about how I feel as how I think?"

She had just said that honesty wasn't the equivalent of giving yourself away, but it was. There was always the safety of a lie.

"No, not really. You're fascinating and attractive, Neill, but—"

His arms were suddenly around her, gathering her body to his. When Joyce was trapped by the hardness of his chest and arms, speechless by his boldness, Neill hesitated. The promise of his mouth hovered right above hers, but he did not kiss her.

It was so deliberate a move, Joyce felt she could read his thoughts. He was challenging her to object and struggle, to say this was not what she wanted. A stab of fear and the pulse of excitement mingled in her stomach. Perhaps she did want this kiss.

The aching moment ended before she found her voice. His lips met hers lightly, like a whisper, until she knew the shape and texture of his mouth. His fingers moved on her back to anchor her, to stroke and play along the soft folds of her blouse. The tip of his tongue ran across her lower lip, a taste of pleasure.

Her heart was beginning to beat too loudly already. A sigh of anticipation threatened to escape, so Joyce held her breath and twisted in his arms to break away.

Neill made no effort to repeat the kiss. He only touched her mouth, still damp and slightly parted, with the end of his forefinger and shook his head almost imperceptibly, as if he were puzzled.

"Is that it? You've had all you want of me, I guess." There was a gently mocking undercurrent in his deep voice.

"You have a terrific reputation as an adventurer—literary, geographic and sexual," Joyce said, getting off the couch as quickly as she could. "You don't have to prove it to me—or with me, Mr. Riordan."

He had carelessly discarded his jacket over one of her chairs. Joyce picked it up and cradled it in her arms, feeling the scratch of wool on the backs of her hands. Neill got her message. He tightened the knot of his tie and a faint smile crossed his face.

"I couldn't resist," he said, standing up and taking a few steps in her direction. "I wanted to kiss you the first night I saw you—before I even knew your name. And when you admit I'm attractive...well, I wasn't aware attraction was a voluntary muscle you can relax or tighten at will."

"I can," snapped Joyce, extending the jacket at the very end of her arm. "I'm not going to get too involved, emotionally or physically, with anyone who is just passing through."

"You could ask me to stay," he retorted, and glanced in the direction of her bedroom.

Her professional poise threatened to give way. A novel wave of shock, outrage and pure amusement overcame her. The man had an ego to match his talent! He probably couldn't imagine a woman immune to his charm or able to resist it.

"Fat chance," muttered Joyce. "I think I'd better re-evaluate my plan and decide if tonight means good night or good-bye. I was trying to explain the need for distance."

"If you keep too far away, you can't see much at all," Neill said. Another secretive smile drew up the corners of his mouth. "It was a grand evening but tonight take the thought of me to bed and see if it warms your sheets."

He actually laughed at the expression on her face as he went to the door and put his hand on the knob. Joyce prudently stayed at the edge of the carpet. There was no way to avoid contact with him in her minuscule foyer. Their bodies would brush each other and the lack of distance would be a problem once more.

"I loved every minute of tonight," Joyce said with a trace of sarcasm. "I hope the magic will hold me for a while, but if I need you—" she snatched up the silver penny whistle "—I'll just whistle. I do know how to whistle."

"And you do look a bit like Lauren Bacall," Neill replied, "but my Bogart imitation leaves a lot to be desired. Call me when you decide if you still want to tackle the task."

He was out the door before Joyce had a chance to react. She stomped around the apartment aimlessly, frustrated by his quick exit and her own anger. She'd blown it—her cool and her chance—and it wasn't like her.

The face reflected in the bathroom mirror, when she scrubbed off her makeup with a vengeance, reminded her of Julia's. *That's whom I'm acting like*, Joyce thought irritably. Her sister was the impulsive, volatile, emotional one. It wasn't easy to decide whether Julia had broken her heart or her pencil, or if her love for Frank was stronger than her commitment to saving baby seals.

As her anger cooled between the chilly sheets of her scrolled brass bed, she thought about Neill's flippant remark. She didn't casually take in a man to warm her thoughts or her linen. And a very unlikely candidate was a man as free-wheeling and unsettling as Neill Riordan.

He was a rule-breaker. He might even be, she decided unprofessionally, a bit nuts. But even so, she couldn't rid her mind of every word he said, the way he looked and moved, the way he held her in his arms.

Two

Joyce shifted the phone from her right ear to her left ear and flipped nervously through the desk calendar's pages until she found today's date. Julia's litany of woe on the other end of the receiver was finally beginning to slow down.

"He's gone," her sister repeated brokenly for the eighteenth time. "I mean, I was absolutely right to tell him to get out...ordering me around, telling me what I should *think*, for the love of... But he went!" Her voice trailed off with a wail and a small hiccough.

"I'm sorry you're so unhappy." Joyce chose the phrase very carefully. She wasn't surprised to hear about Frank's abrupt departure after another round of fighting. She wasn't sure she was sorry he had left.

Both Julia and Frank, her live-in lover, had stormed out of each other's lives regularly over the last few months, only to reconcile. Then, their passionate making up kept them busy until the next hurricane season. Joyce had listened but not interfered; Julia didn't seem very receptive to advice, only consolation.

"What am I going to do?" Julia asked, but the question didn't require a response from Joyce. "I want to spend a few days with you. I'm not going to sit around here, crying and waiting for him to waltz back in or call."

"Okay," agreed Joyce, swallowing her reluctance. She would have suggested Julia examine the reasons for these fights—the blowups occurred over everything from whose night it was to do dishes to disagreements over literary critics—but it was pointless. The reasons didn't matter and they were never resolved. Joyce was the big sister, not Julia's psychologist. "I'm going to be home late this afternoon. I'm taking one of my tykes to Lincoln Park. Lisa's never been to the zoo, if you can believe it.... No, she doesn't want to go."

She chatted on a while longer, not as much for Julia's information as to make sure her sister had calmed down. By the time she hung up, Julia was finished weeping and moaning and Joyce was the one who felt depressed. After an excursion with the reluctant Lisa, a weekend with her moping sister was not a cheery prospect.

"Call me when Lisa arrives," Joyce instructed Margaret. "I don't want to talk to anyone until then."

As if I'm expecting a call, she thought wryly. More than two weeks without a word from Neill and she was still grabbing the phone every time it rang. Well, at least she hadn't called him like an adolescent girl with a crush. Sixteen days and nights and she hadn't given in to the temptation to call and pretend she was interested in more data and not more Neill Riordan.

Joyce's door opened and Lisa stood there, framed in the doorway, shapeless and small in her heavy coat. Her face was wrinkled up in a scowl.

"Ready? Let's go, Prunella Picklepuss," said Joyce with forced gaiety.

"This is a silly idea. I don't want to go," growled Lisa.

Joyce grabbed her coat and purse and took a firm hold on the child's small slack hand. "It's precisely what we both need," insisted Joyce and she added, rather grimly, "It will be fun."

It was a weekday and still too far from spring for most people. Lincoln Park was nearly deserted. A few elderly people braved the wind for the dubious pleasure of March's thin, watery sunshine and each other's company. An occasional energetic rider whizzed by on the bicycle path, but there were more pigeons and squirrels than human visitors.

Lisa scuffed along through the brown leaves and said she was cold. At the single open refreshment stand, she deplored the poor quality of the hot chocolate. While Joyce leaned against the guardrail and applauded the polar bear's water fight, Lisa mentioned spitefully that all zoo animals were atypical, neurotic specimens and not worth studying.

"Could you spare a look?" Joyce asked blandly. She wished she had a text on being a child and having fun. Lisa would pore over it and memorize the salient points but she still wouldn't dream of chasing the pigeons for the sheer delight of seeing them flap away and wheel around the sky and bare-branched trees.

"And now a man is following us," Lisa said in a tentative, uncomfortable voice. She tugged at Joyce's coat and looked back over her shoulder. "He's getting closer. Do you know how many muggers—"

"No one is following us," Joyce began to say, but she broke off her dismissal. As briskly as the breeze, Neill was striding toward them. In a thick white cable-knit sweater and a pair of new jeans, he had his strangely boyish look again. He was red-cheeked from the wind and his walk. Long, wayward curls of his hair hung down across his forehead.

A sharp pressure from Lisa's fingers and Joyce realized she was standing there mutely and the child was genuinely frightened. Neill's size and the determined, slightly ominous set to his features were a little scary.

"He's a friend of mine," Joyce said quickly, giving Lisa his name and a reassuring hug. "What a surprise, Neill! I thought you had classes or seminars every day."

"I have," he said, stopping a few feet from them. He stood there, motionless, and stared raptly at Joyce.

She didn't like his clipped, unusually brief answer, his wide-legged stance or the way he was looking at her. This was hardly the time or place for a show of male aggression, if that's what his defiant posture and tone meant. "Well, then, what are you doing here?" Joyce asked tartly.

"I'm looking for my own cage," retorted Neill. "I've gone as mad as a March hare, so this quest seemed natural enough. You didn't call me."

"I've been busy. I imagine you have, too. I saw your reluctant interview on the *Today Show*. You were very witty, very ascerbic." She became aware of Lisa's head moving like a pendulum from her to Neill and back with the undisguised fascination of a child. She tried signaling Neill by shifting her eyes down to Lisa and softening her own voice. "Well, it's been a while."

"Only a while, is it? A taste of eternity. I actually begged your cruel secretary for a word with you. Finally, I told her I was a desperate man about to do a desperate act and I would name her responsible in my final note if she didn't put me through instantly."

"Poor Margaret," murmured Joyce.

"Hang poor Margaret," thundered Neill. "Poor me!"

Lisa gave a little jump at the bellowing and Joyce said, "Neill," in shrill reproof. He glanced down and saw the wide-eyed girl as if she had just materialized. Joyce took a step away from him and found Lisa had become rooted to the path.

"I'm Irish and excitable. Your pardon, darling," Neill was saying to Lisa.

"I thought you were a mugger. Then I thought you were drunk. Do you always talk that way?"

"I wish I were drunk, but I'm not. It's not sobriety or a lack of it bothering me, but the spring. The sap is rising in me, perhaps." He gave Joyce a sidelong look and beamed at Lisa. "Look around, girl. Something is happening to all the creatures here...."

"Neill," admonished Joyce. She was not prepared to listen to an impromptu sex education lecture.

"I know all about that stuff," reported the eight-year-old, and she actually smiled at Neill. "What I don't know is why anyone would want to come to a zoo."

"Well, let me see," he mused, moving smoothly between Joyce and Lisa and taking their hands. "Some folks think it's to feel superior to other animals. We put them in cages and think we are the better animals, don't we? Shall it be the lions or the great apes next?"

"Let's leave," suggested Lisa.

"Fine, the lions." He laughed, pulling Joyce closer to him and setting off at a fast pace. Lisa had to stretch her legs to keep up and soon got too breathless to continue her argument that the zoo was a waste of time.

"Does it work on little girls, too?" Joyce asked him softly as he offered to race them up the stairs of the lion house. He gave her a smile of radiant innocence. "The blarney, the Irish baloney, Neill," she clarified. "Are you really irresistible to all females, regardless of age?"

"*You* didn't call," he said.

But I wanted to, she thought shakily. His face was close enough for her to see a shaving nick, to get the full effect of his own special scent and to remember how his mouth felt when it was on hers.

"It stinks in here," announced Lisa loudly. "Can we go now?"

Neill suggested to Lisa that she had the wrong viewpoint for seeing lions. He told her to watch the animals and instead of thinking what they meant—or didn't mean—to her, she ought to guess what the lions and tigers were thinking about her. "I want a full report," he said, sending her ahead of them.

Lisa seemed delighted with the suggestion, and raced through the huge, vaulted building to the opposite exit. She dashed off with a brief, obedient glance into each cage while Neill held Joyce's hand and arm firmly under his own, keeping her with him.

"What a little old lady, she is," chuckled Neill. He turned Joyce to the rail and put his arm around her back. For a while he said nothing else, and they watched the panther pace restlessly, endlessly, around the perimeter of his cage. "Look, when he moves and the light catches him right, you can see his markings even in the blackness of the fur."

The panther stopped and fastened his liquid-fire eyes on them. Joyce was acutely aware of the weight of Neill's arm, the length of his body along hers. "I don't think this is a good idea," she said.

"Nonsense, I love the zoo. It's a fine idea."

"You know what I mean." Joyce saw the panther resume his measured, stately walk and avoided both the gray eyes and the golden ones. She waved at Lisa at the far end of the building and moved with Neill to the next cage.

His ungloved fingers were still chilly when he lifted them and touched her face. "I want to keep seeing you and I had to come today to tell you that," Neill said quietly. "This place is very appropriate because I don't want to be only a creature you're studying, a new variety of leopard or bird or man. The other night, the last time I saw you, I wasn't. Why are you putting up bars between us?"

"I'm not," Joyce denied too vigorously. "There are limits on any relationship, and I can see them, that's all. I don't just go with my feelings or impulses."

She could have told him so much more. Sixteen days was a long time to think about a man she didn't expect to see again. He was like the leopard in some ways: exciting, dangerous, ready to pounce and very quick. He was not the kind of man a woman would trust or care too much for if she wanted to survive. She could have told him, but he didn't give her a chance.

His fingers slid deep into her hair and he pulled her to him, kissing her with a private hunger in a very public place. There was no chance to protest, and soon Joyce didn't want to protest. The limits she could see clearly a few seconds ago had blurred; there was only the soft fire of his mouth, the press of his body and the answering heat that flared in her.

This kiss was not a question; it was a statement. His lips moved on hers, hard, and then lighter, sweeter, daring her to break the contact, and she couldn't. It felt so good to lean into him, so exciting to drink in the warm pleasure of his kiss and let the wild feeling rise and spread. And Joyce could not pretend it was his madness, his desire spilling into her. She wanted more. She burned to touch more of him. Her fingertips itched to move over smooth skin, hard muscle, not through the softness of his sweater.

She heard, dimly, the roar of a lion and a faint, nervous laugh. The roar might be the echo of her blood; the laughter might be the trembling inside her, but it wasn't. Neill's lips eased on hers, taking small, gentle kisses with him. His face came slowly back into focus.

One of the elderly regulars who haunted the lion house for warmth laughed again and leaned over for a conference with his companion. Unable to think of anything to say to Neill that would not embarrass her even more, Joyce glanced around for Lisa. He had been right about eloquence without words; she had already said too much. Apparently, Lisa was the only one in the building who missed their show. The child was standing with her nose flat against the glass-walled exhibit of cubs when Joyce, with Neill trailing her, reached her side.

"Did you try what I told you?" Neill inquired, and Lisa nodded up and down without taking her eyes off the fat-bellied lion cub and his keeper. "Well, what are they thinking of us?"

"That we're slow and fat and good to eat, except for kids like me. I'm too small and skinny." She gave Neill an appraising look. "You're about the size they'd like. A big zebra-size person."

It was the first hint of whimsy or imagination Joyce had even seen in the girl, and she followed it up quickly. What did the big cats think about the daily parade of visitors? What kinds of people looked tastier? What did the cub think about, cradled in a human's arms and drinking messily from a bottle?

"Oh, he's different," Lisa said with a trace of wistfulness. "He isn't like the lions who were born in Africa. If I could take him home with me and..." She didn't finish her thought.

"Play with him?" prodded Joyce gently. Lisa's world was full of adults who talked to her and treated her like a miniature adult. Something or someone small and helpless might be what she needed. "Tickle his tummy like the man is doing?"

"Yes," nodded Lisa with a smile curving the corners of her usually pinched, tight little mouth. The cub was biting energetically at his khaki-clad attendant's fingers, shirt collar, and then swiping at his face with a rough pink tongue.

"Most leases don't allow lions in the apartment and that cub is going to get awfully big and strong very quickly," Joyce teased. "How about a kitten?" She made a mental note to speak to Lisa's mother about a pet.

The moment of childishness had passed for Lisa. She made some reply about the destructive nature of cats and started for the exit, but Joyce wasn't fooled. The interest was there and the incident satisfied Joyce. Lisa might very well respond emotionally to a kitten and find out there was nothing wrong with fun and play and silly, warm shows of affection—toward animals or people.

"I could do with a bit of tickling," Neill whispered into Joyce's ear. "I don't scratch the drapes or tear at the furniture. Will you take me home with you?" He made a low growling sound in his throat and lifted her hand to his mouth. Then, very delicately and deliberately, he licked at the base of her thumb.

It was a slow, tantalizing gesture and Joyce felt her desire for him stir. His tender, intimate touch fired her imagination. He would make love to her, given the chance, like that. An unhurried, intense lover, Neill would find all the sensitive spots. He had the obvious eye, as well as ear, for giving and getting pleasure.

"I...I can't," Joyce said. Julia would be there for who knew how long. It wasn't fair to offer her sister a shoulder to cry on, a quiet place to put herself together, and then bring Neill home. She explained the problem between Frank and Julia briefly and how rarely Julia asked for help or comfort or advice.

Neill twisted an errant strand of her gold hair idly before pushing it behind her ear. His finger traced the curve of her ear, the slope of her cheek, and came to rest at the very edge of her lip. "And, I take it, that means you won't come with me?"

"No, I won't," Joyce murmured. It was much too soon to feel the pangs of regret and frustration, but she did. There was such longing in his eyes, and it mirrored her own feeling. He wanted her, she wanted him, and Neill had a way of making what was incredibly complex seem absurdly simple.

"Ah, well, spring will come soon enough," he said, almost as if he were talking to himself. "To everything there is a season.... Now, where is your little friend?"

"Watching us." Joyce shaded her eyes with her hand and looked down the long, blacktopped path. Lisa was in front of the ape house, arranged on the low concrete wall in a calculated pose of impatience. "She probably finds our behavior sillier and more pointless than the animals."

Neill laughed and put his arm firmly around Joyce's waist. "Probably so, but she's a child, not a poet."

After three days of listening to Julia, Joyce was tired. Work took its normal, expected toll and Julia took up the evenings. Between eating everything that wasn't nailed down, Julia went over her relationship with Frank in graphic detail, enumerating all his shortcomings and all her weaknesses. It was exhausting emotionally and getting expensive—with nightly stops at the supermarket—but Joyce had thought her sister was showing some real maturity and some genuine insight, until Frank appeared at the door.

"I need you, Julia," he had said, and with those four words three whole nights of soul-searching and breast-beating flew out the window.

"Are you mad at me?" Julia asked Joyce as she threw all her clothes back into a duffel bag. She stuffed in the last of a package of Oreos and looked apologetically at Joyce.

"I'm annoyed, yes. And I'm confused." Joyce heard Frank's voice in the living room and realized he was talking back to the television, disagreeing with the news announcer. She shut her bedroom door. "After everything you said, after all that analysis of why you and he are not compatible, he says 'jump' and you're in the air again."

"You don't understand," Julia said. "I can't stand it when he tells me what to do and we end up fighting. But he was asking me to come back, Joyce. He does need me! Oh, I was right about him being stubborn and unyielding and opinionated to the point of insanity but—"

"But? I really don't understand now." Joyce let the anger out finally. "You like living in a powderkeg, is that it? He's the steel that strikes sparks off you and the next explosion is always minutes away. Those are your words, not mine."

"If you loved someone, you'd understand," Julia said rather smugly. "You and I are as different as sisters can be and we always have been. We fought like cats and dogs but we are also lots closer than some sisters because we love each other. If you ever feel about a man the way I feel about Frank, you'll understand."

Feeling sick and tired, Joyce didn't bother offering any further arguments. There was nothing more to say if Julia wanted to believe love excused all faults and overcame reason. She was grateful she had never been as blind and besotted by a man and hoped she never would be.

They left in a tangle of arms and legs, reunited once more. Stoic, stolid Frank was nuzzling Julia and breathing inaudible things. Endearments and promises tonight, Joyce thought wearily, but not for long. She closed the door and relaxed on the couch. The silence surrounded her like a welcome blanket.

When Neill called, as he had every night for the last three, she was limp and dulled with sleep. He sounded strange, his lovely voice thick and coarsened, but for a minute or so what he said could not penetrate the groggy mist she was wrapped in.

"I'm dying," he repeated. There was a very convincing spate of coughing and wheezing. "I hurt like a man who's been beaten. Do you care?"

"Of course I care," Joyce said. She sat up so fast, her head swam. "Oh, Neill, it's no wonder you're sick. Running around without a coat or hat. Have you called a doctor?"

"You," he croaked. "I'm never sick and I hate doctors. I must be dying."

She didn't know quite whether to laugh or cry. He really was the most exasperating man. He sounded so awful that she could believe his diagnosis and yet, a suspicion nagged at her. "What do you want me to do? I'm not an M.D., Neill. Shall I call my internist of the University Health Service for you?"

There was a long pause during which she could hear his labored breathing. "Dammit, I can find the strength to dial a phone, as you can see," Neill said, and both pain and anger were clear in his tone. "It's you I want and you I need, Joyce."

"Neill..." She realized immediately that the phone was dead but she sat there clutching it in a daze. Of course, he was being ridiculous. He was as strong as a bull and not very likely to die of a cold. A heaviness gripped Joyce as she tried unsuccessfully to call him back for over an hour. She paced, tethered to the phone, while a busy signal whined in her ear.

Every time she thought she had sorted him out and knew who Neill Riordan was, he surprised her. She knew Neill when he was lighthearted or serious or even tender, but she had not expected him to have a weak, vulnerable side. If this was a game of his, Joyce decided as she threw an odd assortment of articles in a brown paper bag, she would kill him herself.

She risked a speeding ticket on the outer drive and parked illegally near his house. The front door was unlocked; Neill couldn't seem to understand that Chicago was not a rural Irish village where an unlatched door was a sign of manners and hospitality. Joyce had not been inside before, but one glance around her sufficed.

The house was cold and a shambles. It didn't look dirty, just totally chaotic. Every table and chair was stacked with books and papers, the dining room table was covered with his laundry, and the kitchen was obviously his writing room and nothing more. Joyce found the thermostat, gaped at the setting and turned on the furnace. She stood at the bottom of the stairs and called his name without getting a response.

He was sleeping, surrounded by more books and covered only with a sheet. His forehead and upper lip were beaded with sweat and Joyce could see the sheen on his chest and throat. One long, muscular leg was thrust out from beneath the rumpled sheet and although Joyce felt like a voyeur, she could not stop herself from appreciating the sight of him. For a man of letters who lived by his wits, Neill was muscular and well-developed. Even relaxed, there was a roundness to his arms, a rise of his thigh muscle.

Joyce went quietly to his bedside and tried to draw the sheet up around him and clear some of the books off the bed. She could feel the heat of fever rising from him, and when his eyes opened, glass-bright and puzzled, she pushed the damp strands of hair back from his forehead.

"I'm delirious," Neill said, "and dreaming. Maybe I've died and there is a heaven." He struggled upright and the sheet fell away alarmingly. The movement set off a fit of coughing, and Joyce pushed him back on the pillows.

"You must have the flu. I brought the cure."

Neill smiled faintly and patted the bed next to himself. "I believe you have. I feel better already."

She gave him a dirty look and opened the brown paper bag, holding up each item in turn. "Aspirin, chicken noodle soup, frozen orange juice, a Snoopy coloring book with only one page done, some comic books. I'll go downstairs and see if I can find a pan to heat the soup in and you put on some pajamas."

"Don't have any," Neill said weakly but happily. "Why did you come?"

Joyce pulled the box of crayons out of the bottom of the bag and tossed them on top of the coloring book. She took her purse and the red and white can of soup and started to cross the room. "I don't know. I guess I was afraid it was a sin to let an Irishman die before St. Patrick's Day. You're supposed to march in the parade."

"You care," Neill said as loudly as he could. "I'm a lovable rogue and you can't help yourself. I knew we were fated to be friends and lovers." He groaned and rubbed his chest and ribs, contenting himself with a lingering look at her breasts. "If I don't die...."

Joyce marched downstairs, and as her foot hit each tread she offered another adjective to the empty air. "Arrogant, insufferable, crazy, self-centered..." There was a whole flight of stairs and she managed to find a word to describe Neill for every step. But she could not add *liar* to her list.

Three

It took a certain genius to make a simple bowl of soup in Neill's kitchen. The can opener was in the vegetable crisper, the silverware was all in one place but not, unfortunately, in a drawer and a pot required a room-to-room search. Joyce was used to eccentric ideas of organization by her young patients. But Neill had refined the eccentric to an art.

When she had managed her culinary best, Joyce balanced the saucepan of soup, spoon and crackers on a turkey platter and carried it up to him.

"No bowls?" she inquired. "From the looks of it, you exist on cornflakes, sardines in mustard sauce and mango chutney. It's no wonder you're sick."

Neill smiled wanly. "I hate mango chutney. A student gave it to me." He took the platter without comment and dutifully started in on the soup.

Joyce leaned up against the doorframe and told him about Brian Wiggins, who was subsisting solely on a strict diet of cream cheese and bacon sandwiches. "His mother brought him to the Bennett for behavior modification three months ago and he's been working with me."

"Having any success?" Neill was genuinely interested. He slowed the rhythm of his spoon. "You've never told me much about my miniature counterparts."

"Confidentiality," Joyce said, pulling a mock-serious face. "I don't think Brian would mind if I let you in on the results. He's gained five pounds, is apparently thriving and made a convert. I love cream cheese and bacon and Brian."

Neill finished and pushed the platter aside. "You really like children," he commented. "It's not fashionable, you know. Bright or not, they're usually viewed as selfish, annoying pests."

"That's because I don't view them. I talk with them, interact with them."

"Tell me about some of the others," demanded Neill. "You don't have to name them or give me their I.Q. scores. I'm sure they all could speak in four dead languages and figure the national deficit before they walked."

She didn't resent his interest or his questions tonight. For one thing, she wasn't the focus of his inquiry. It was always nice when someone was an impressed with the spectrum of her patients as she was. She didn't have the sense that Neill was idly curious or looking for a topic to divert himself while he was feeling awful.

He laughed with her over her patient dubbed "the great mouth," who had not yet found a school ready for his spontaneous, outrageous and continual commentary. Joyce saw real concern flicker across Neill's face when she described some of the more serious problems.

"Is running away common?" he asked. "Is that why you're always after me for all the gory details of my escapades?"

"That's why and it's not unusual," answered Joyce honestly. Neill yawned and she couldn't help following his lead. "I'm tiring you out. We can talk about kids who want to turn into computers or blow up their basements some other time."

"I ache. I feel as if I were dragged through a keyhole and back."

He shifted uncomfortably on the bed and Joyce went to help him move the pillows. In the golden light of his lamp, she could see the creased lines of fatigue and the shadows of pain on his face. It bothered her to see him suddenly so vulnerable and alone. When Neill was all self-assurance and strength, she could resist him. When he looked and sounded less sure of himself, Joyce found herself wanting to ease and soothe him.

It would have been nicer if her feelings were just friendly, all innocent, even maternal. They weren't. Neill moved, raised one knee, turning slightly toward her. She was conscious of how smoothly his muscles worked under the skin, how the shaded light made the hairs on his forearms glitter, how thin the sheet was. Florence Nightingale would not have found a man's navel or an exposed lean stretch of hip as interesting.

Her hand reached to touch his brow, to check once more before she left. She stopped herself, suddenly unwilling to touch him, and asked Neill if there was a thermometer anywhere.

"In there." He thrust his chin toward the bathroom. "I saw one in the medicine cabinet."

His eyes took in her awkward pose, hand poised in mid-air, and flicked up to her face. Joyce went and made a show of cabinet-rummaging for a few minutes, grateful that he had resisted a quip or comment at her reluctance.

As she came back in the room, Joyce felt him watching her every step. She extended the thermometer and the second she got close enough, Joyce thrust it into his mouth.

"Under your tongue," she ordered when Neill waggled his eyebrows and the thermometer at her. "No talking, one full minute."

Unfortunately, she couldn't order him to close his eyes. Sixty seconds of silence was very long under an unblinking, unwavering stare. Her own pulse rate sped up a little.

"You'll live. Your temperature is high but not alarming." Joyce stopped squinting at the silver column of mercury and put the thermometer on his bedside table. "Now, I'll take the dishes to the kitchen, wash up and leave you to sleep."

"Stay," Neill demanded and then added, "Please. I want you to stay, Joyce."

"You'll be fine," she assured him, stacking the saucepan and silverware on a tray. "Julia and Frank live closer than I do. I can have her stop by tomorrow morning...."

He caught her wrist and held it. His fever might be dropping, but Joyce was startled by the scorching heat of his fingers on her. "I called *you*. You were my nurse—or doctor—or companion of choice. Stay and talk to me. Read to me if you want to. But stay."

She knew he really should just sleep, but this unexpected opportunity to be with him tempted her. He didn't seem to be in any condition to make a pass at her tonight. Maybe in a weakened state Neill would be willing to talk, not banter or argue, and tell her exactly what she needed to know.

"For a while," she agreed slowly. "Until you fall asleep, okay?"

"Fine." His grin revealed the small gap between his front teeth and he looked boyishly pleased.

"Now, let me go and you color or read one of the comic books."

His fingers unwound from her wrist reluctantly. She could still feel their imprint on her skin and his eyes watching her when she left the room. When she came back, he was looking haggard but happy and he swept aside papers and books with his arm to clear a space on the bed for Joyce.

She hesitated. There was no other place to sit, really, but it was disconcerting to think about chatting away, perched next to his barely clad form.

"Oh, come on," Neill said, chiding Joyce for thoughts she hadn't even expressed. "I'm as weak and helpless as a baby. I can't even find my red crayon by myself."

He patted the sheets and the white linen slipped downward until he adjusted it.

"You're very safe with me tonight," he added when she settled herself next to him. "Can I hope for a back rub? A search for the crayon, at least?"

"Cute. Very cute." Joyce laughed and shook her head in disbelief. "You can hope for company and if you don't follow doctor's orders, you can expect me to go."

"I don't know why you go on resisting me," Neill teased. He ran his hands up and down under the sheets until he held up the red crayon in triumph. "You like me. You came all the way over to save my life, so you do care."

"I care. I'm risking a good case of the flu for you. Take your aspirin and tell me why a healthy man thought he was dying a few hours ago."

"Because I'm almost never sick," Neill said. "Because I'm afraid to die before I've done my best..."

She glanced over at him when he broke off abruptly and Neill was lost in some private thought. As open and extroverted as Neill could be, there were secret places he had that no one could find. He looked not only pale now but troubled. Joyce touched his upper arm lightly and his face turned toward hers, his eyes very dark.

"What's wrong?" she asked quietly. "Are you feeling worse?"

"Worse and better, all at once," Neill replied hoarsely. "You've wanted me to talk about my past, to dwell on it. I've just seen the present up close and glimpsed the future."

"I don't understand." The intensity of his look and his words frightened Joyce a little. Was he delirious? Was there any truth in the rumors of his talent being touched with madness?

"I love you." Neill tested the sound of the words as he spoke slowly. "I knew I wanted you but this is different. I called you tonight because I wanted you close. Not to make love to, not even to nurse me, but simply to be here."

"I'll pretend I didn't hear that," Joyce said. "And you'll thank me in the morning. Love doesn't happen like this— in such a short time, between people as different, as unsuited to each other. It's absurd."

"Love is absurd?" He touched her cheek and ran his finger down to her chin, down the line of her throat and let it rest in the small hollow at its base.

"Of course not," she corrected. "I meant, it's too soon to decide such a thing and it's too unlikely to be real."

"Really?" He reached up and slid his hand under the weight of her hair, rubbing the nape of her neck. "I suppose there is some psychological formula to figure out the optimum time to fall in love. Or is it a checklist you fill out?"

Joyce fixed her eyes straight ahead and folded her arms tightly across her midsection. The pressure against her ribs did not quell the strange flutter in her stomach or make her forget the tingling spreading down her back from his massaging fingers. Something was very wrong; he was the one with the flu and she was feeling weak.

"There's attraction, infatuation and lust, for starters," Joyce said, putting as much authority as she could in her voice. "I'm sure you've had experience with all those very natural expressions of your sexuality before."

"I have," he answered. "Have you?"

"I'm uneasy with the direction our conversation is taking," Joyce whispered. "I should warn you, Neill. I'm not above using whatever romantic illusions you are harboring to get you to agree to see me on a regular basis. I want to do this study, not go to bed with you."

"You are in bed with me." His chuckle broke off in a cough. "And you are welcome to use me any way you see fit. I'm showing admirable restraint, aren't I?"

His whole body slid closer to her, the length of his leg coming to rest next to hers. Joyce glanced over, exasperated, and had to suppress an exclamation. "You are showing more than restraint. I'm afraid the mystery is gone."

Before Neill could hoist the sheet, she got up and went to find a blanket. The quip had come easily, but she felt herself flushed and uncomfortable. Neill was wheezing faintly from behind her and she hoped it was from congestion, not amusement. He had noticed her looking a little too long and a little too appreciatively at his inadvertent but inviting exhibitionism.

"What a great place to store blankets," she commented, returning with a thick comforter. "Very few people keep them on the floor of the closets in winter."

"I like it cool. Not this cold, but cool." Neill's voice sounded peculiar again. "Clara Barton to the rescue."

She spread the quilt over him, tucking it under his arms, over his chest, as if she were the model of nursing efficiency. Neill reached up and tugged her down next to him.

"Talk," he ordered as if he had guessed her intention to go downstairs and call the university hospital. He mumbled something else Joyce couldn't catch because of the chattering of his teeth.

"All right," she said with resignation. "Close your eyes and try to go to sleep." Having exhausted her anecdotes about her clients was no problem. She could lull him to quiet with the uneventful story of her own life.

There was method to the madness, she thought smugly as her voice hit an even, soothing drone. Whatever prompted his declaration of love would be cooled by her undramatic and unglamorous recital. She could show him how hopelessly far apart they were by simply being as honest and open with Neill as she wanted him to be with her.

"...A comfortable middle-class family in a suburb...good grades but no scholarship...no wild rebellion as a teen...love working at the Bennett and I'll stay as long as they'll have me...."

It was easier when his powerful smoky eyes were closed. When the rise and fall of the comforter across his broad chest became more regular, she smiled to herself.

"The only tragedy in my life is that there have been no great tragedies or triumphs." She made a wry face and put her feet up, pushing a sharp-edged book aside. "Dealing with the kids is a series of small steps forward and backward and there's no blinding light to signal success."

There wasn't a sound from Neill except the deep, rhythmic breathing. Joyce eyed the doorway and decided to give it a few more minutes. She put her head back, looked up at the ceiling and yawned. She didn't even censor herself when she mentioned her engagement three years ago.

Neill certainly wouldn't be shocked, and she wanted him to know she wasn't entirely inexperienced in matters of love. Just because it hadn't evolved into marriage didn't mean she was ignorant about a mature, warm relationship. That's what she meant by love, not fireworks and cymbals clashing.

"Hardly inspiring," she murmured, "and except for the normal crisis here and there, nothing anyone would write about. I think *average* says it all."

"Don't bet on it," said Neill hoarsely. He turned on his side toward her and one long arm closed over her. He did not open his eyes. "Go on, I'm listening."

His move was anything but predatory. Joyce let his arm encircle her waist and she kept talking. It was more than the fatigue of the day and the exhaustion of Julia's stay catching up with her. It felt good. It didn't even feel strange, lying next to Neill, saying whatever came into her head, as if they had reversed roles.

"Maybe that's why I got hooked on exploring brilliant minds," Joyce ended sleepily. "I grew up here, where I was planted, not branching out, not moving in fits and starts, or hitting every high and low. Unlike you, I just want to understand..."

Her own heavy-lidded eyes refused to say open another second. She felt Neill's body move slightly and the room was suddenly plunged into darkness when he snapped off the lamp. Instead of the nearness and the pressure of his body making her tense, Joyce found she was limp, drained of any desire to leave.

From shoulder to calf, Neill nestled against her and she had almost forgotten how warm and companionable it felt to share space in a bed and confidences in the night. There was nothing aggressive or threatening in the way he held her to himself, just an affectionate closeness. Joyce hadn't planned the night, hadn't planned to reveal so much about herself, but she realized she was glad it happened.

Friends, she thought, slipping into sleep. They had begun to forge a friendship and that would be fine. She could trust him as a friend, work with him as a friend, and no one would get hurt. He had even said she could use him any way she wanted. *I'll hold him to that in the morning.*

Neill woke, expecting to find her curled next to him, anticipating more of the same delicious torture of last night. He was only sick, not dying, as her presence had proved. It had required a saintly disposition to lie there sleepless and aching from more than a virus and do nothing, say nothing. He knew he was no saint. This morning there were no tempting, rounded curves snug against him. The scent of her perfume was there but fainter than when he had pressed his face to her hair and drawn in the rich, intoxicating fragrance of a woman he wanted, a woman he loved.

He opened his eyes without raising his head. Joyce was asleep on her back, one knee slightly raised and one hand outstretched toward him, the other on her stomach. The ribbed banding of her sweater was worked upward, leaving bare a strip of skin so pale and fragile-looking, Neill thought of the translucent beauty of a child's flesh.

It had been a mistake to tell her what he was thinking last night. After all these years, he should be used to seeing the anger or disbelief in other eyes when he said the unexpected, the truths he felt. Joyce had not laughed or punched him but she wanted to pretend he had not said it. *I love you.* Those blue lakes of her eyes turned away, dismissed him. She did not understand, yet, but she wanted to.

Neill propped himself up on his elbows to see the way the fine tendrils of blond hair clung to the side of her face, her cheek, like feathers. There was a pulse beat at the base of her arched white throat. Someday he would tell her about the ancient sea god, Lir, and his children who were transformed to swans. She might like the Celtic legend, but she would think he was crazy if he compared her to one of those enchanted creatures.

He never disputed anyone, including the critics, when they said he was crazy. No one in his right mind would choose to be a poet; it was like aspiring to be the high priest of a little-practiced, outdated religion. Poetry had made him a curiosity and an outcast and, finally, almost a celebrity. Being a poet was not an honest, secure life with regular hours and good health benefits.

And she'd want that in her man, Neill thought, reaching over very cautiously to free a strand of her hair from the corner of her mouth. Why else would she suddenly tell him about how smooth, how straight, how ordinary her path had been if not to let him know they were worlds apart? She liked what she had and he was the unknown—an unsafe, erratic man.

Joyce's hand flexed. Her lips parted and closed mutely and Neill hoped it was a dream he played some part in, not one with a stockbroker in a tailored three-piece suit. He wished he could reach over and take up the invitation of her mouth once more and find her willing. She was not ordinary in any way except she did not understand that there was a magical tie between them. *Magic* was not a term found in any of her psychology texts.

Only poets wrote about love, and only young children believed in magic. He would have to be patient and show her. If all she wanted now from him was talk, she could have it. If all she ever wanted was talk, there was no way she would know what was missing from a life of plans and rules.

"Oh, no," Joyce gasped, her eyelids flickering open. She sat up slowly amid the rumpled bedclothes and books, and rubbed her forehead. "I was having the weirdest dream. That's what you get from sleeping fully clothed in a strange bed on top of—" she pulled a leather-bound volume from underneath her and peered at the spine "—Thomas Moore?"

"Another poet, very Irish and long gone," said Neill. "Nobody reads him anymore, I suspect, and he's obviously no fun to sleep with. Well, neither was I, for that matter."

"I'll never tell," Joyce kidded him, "if you won't." She checked her watch and got up with the lithe, fluid grace Neill associated with her every movement. "Look, Neill, I'll see if I can make some breakfast in this library or go out and find an open coffee shop. Then, if you're going to be all right, I've got to get home. There's a ton of work to catch up on and Julia's finally gone."

"I'll need constant care. You better plan to stay a week," Neill said. "We can start those regular meetings today. What time is it?"

"Nine. A little after nine." She grabbed her purse and started for the door with a promise she would call. Next week would be soon enough for sessions, she assured him. "Breakfast and I'm off, okay?"

Neill smiled. "No problem. Just do me the favor of telling my tutorial students that I'm not in shape today." He folded his arms across his chest and gave Joyce a lingering, appraising look. "They know I don't lock the house. They're probably down there right now, wondering what's keeping me. When you come waltzing down the stairs, no further explanation will be needed."

Joyce met his eyes squarely. "I don't embarrass that easily, Neill, and I don't quit. Now that I've won a concession from you—no more fly-by-night get-togethers—I won't give up until the study's done."

"God, I hope not, love," Neill said quietly but clearly. "Neither will I."

Four

Joyce supposed she had won, but the phrase "*cold comfort*" kept popping into her mind. She was meeting with Neill regularly enough. Three times this week, she mentally toted up. Her colleagues would have thought she was crazy if they knew the circumstances.

"I think better and talk more when I'm doing something outdoors—walking, eating, sight-seeing," Neill announced, and Joyce didn't have much choice but to compromise. She suggested a stroll through the Art Institute today and was overruled. A walk along windy Navy Pier was almost useless. Half of her questions blew away. Most of his remarks were hard to hear over the chattering of her teeth.

"Had enough for today?" Neill slapped his gloved hand on the steel railing and looked away from the darkening sky and gray-green Lake Michigan. "You know more about me now than my own mother. I conveniently forgot to tell her about all my troubles at Trinity College; she fancied the notion that they were making me into a gentleman as well as a scholar."

"They have turned out lots of famous writers but I suspect working miracles was beyond them." Joyce pulled her head down as far as it would go into the collar of her coat and peeked out at Neill. Her nose and cheeks were bright red and the wind made her eyes tear.

"Poor turtle!" He put his arm around her and gave her a hard squeeze. "You've had a full day of your muddled children and two hours of Riordan's rantings and ravings. Want to give up?"

"I want to be warm," rasped Joyce. "I think you're trying to wear me down, Neill. I've listened to your life story, trailing you through the streets of Chicago. I've discussed your philosophy over some Irish jigs and reels in that park performance you dragged me to."

"You didn't like the music?" Neill snorted with sudden laughter, and ruffled her already windblown hair. "Next, you'll tell me you hated the fish and the tea and you didn't care for those nice countrymen of mine we met."

"The fish was greasy. The tea was so strong, it could dissolve the enamel off teeth, and I thought Shea and Mallory were going to come to blows." Joyce shuddered with a fresh gust of wind and the memory. It was impossible to maintain rapport when two strangers invited themselves over and got embroiled in a shouting match over politics. "You probably hope I'm getting discouraged...or too frozen to keep going. I won't give up. Not with the weirdest kid they assign to me or with you, either. I'll finish this study if I have to climb the Water Tower to interview you."

"That's the spirit," encouraged Neill cheerfully. He pressed Joyce's head into the front of his jacket as the wind whistled around the corner, assaulting them. "I like a fighter. I just can't seem to walk away from trouble myself."

She glared balefully at him before she ducked into her car, and took her time reaching over to unlock his side. Chicago's blustery weather didn't bother him. Running an obstacle course, mental and physical, after his full day of teaching and writing, didn't bother him. He was the most intense, energetic man she'd ever met and, despite her best efforts to stay aloof and uninvolved, she was aware of liking him more and more.

Neill talked to everyone. He would stop on the street and chat animatedly with someone and only later would Joyce learn he'd never met the person before. He talked to everyone but confided in very few. She could see in his face, and in the taut line of his jaw, how hard it was for him to trust her with the painful memories of a poor childhood, the systematic attempts of family and school and even the law to make him obey and conform.

He was born for trouble. His stories of childhood poverty and growing up in a bare-bones, bare-knuckle environment were bleak and told with a minimum of fuss. She still didn't know why nothing had ever broken his spirit. Given his background, Neill's emergence as a person, let alone a poet, was on the order of a miracle.

By the time he was fifteen, Neill had covered Ireland on foot from one end to the other. He wasn't sure what drove him, and he laughed when she suggested her psychology expertise could offer an answer. "Hocus-pocus" Neill called her field, but then he referred to his own works as "scribbling".

With a life of comfort and ease—the kind of protected world she and Julia and most of her patients had—what would Neill have done? He seemed to thrive on trouble.

She couldn't think of anyone else who could make the leap from a Borstal, a boys' prison, to Trinity College on scholarship.

"When was the last time you were arrested?" Joyce asked offhandedly. The traffic was too heavy for her to look over at him safely, but she knew he was watching her, not the scenery. Neill's habit of staring at her as if they'd just met was duly noted in her journal.

"Ah, let's see. California. In Los Angeles I took a photographer's camera away from him and he charged me with assault. The charges were dismissed."

"Didn't want him to steal your spirit by taking a snapshot? Was that it?" She was teasing, but sometimes it was an effective way to get him to talk.

There was a hesitation, longer than most pauses in their conversations lately. "I was with a lady who was not eager to have her picture taken."

Her inner voice told her to leave it there. Asking about Neill's romantic escapades wasn't, by any stretch of the imagination, going to yield data on the etiology of his genius. If she probed in certain areas, she'd have to accept the fact that she was asking for herself.

"A student?" Joyce thought about seeing Neill that first night, reading to his students. The worshipful faces were tilted up at him for a ray of light. Julia had painted him verbally as if he were Adonis and Chaucer rolled up into one package.

She braked for a red light and took the opportunity to glance over at him. He was smiling at her, a pleased, slightly knowing smile that wrinkled the corners of his eyes.

"If you're interested, I'll tell you," he said softly. "It's fair, after all. You did mention the grand passion of your life to me...an affair to remember. I forget your fiancé's name, forgive me."

"I *never* told you," Joyce said hotly. The light changed and the driver behind her hit his horn at precisely the same time. She took a tighter grip on the wheel and her emotions.

"Not a student," Neill said abruptly.

Joyce made a small gesture with one hand, a wave as if she were brushing away a fly. "I shouldn't have asked. It's none of my business unless it relates to your formative years."

"It related to lust, not love."

"I'm not asking."

"I have a wide acquaintance with lust," Neill went on, undaunted. "Love was a complete mystery until this January. I saw your eyes first—wide and wary but filled with a strength. Then a firm handshake and those impossibly small wrists, skin like fresh cream. A diamond-hard mind encased in white velvet."

The warmth in her toes had nothing to do with the car's heater.

If it cost Neill to confide, she was paying a price, too. He was insinuating himself into her feelings, her thoughts, her dreams. His fierce independence touched her, but Neill did not. He would take her hand, give her a companionable hug or shield her from the wind, but it was not a prelude to more touching, another kiss. She wanted him as a friend and he was accommodating her. Why did it bother her so much? She wanted to see him on a friendly basis and he'd granted her wish. Why didn't the moments of electric tension go away and the gnawing, nagging attraction disappear?

"Drop me here, love. I have some more walking to do." Neill indicated a corner miles from his house.

Joyce double-parked and asked no more questions. Neill walked from one end of the city to the other when he was working on a poem or a lecture or a problem. It was a minor and healthy characteristic except that he did it at all hours, night and day, in randomly chosen journeys through any neighborhood.

"It's cold. Don't you want to have coffee somewhere?"

"I will," he replied, opening the car door.

"I meant with me," offered Joyce. "I wouldn't mind as long as we can sit down and stop this imitation of perpetual motion. I feel like I'm training for a marathon."

He half-turned, leaning toward her. Her hand tightened on the steering wheel and there was an unmistakable flow of anticipation in her veins. He was going to kiss her. He was, and she wasn't sure she wouldn't kiss him back.

"I've had my ration of Joyce for today," Neill said very slowly. "A little more, a little closer in a quiet place, and I might get greedy again."

"Oh," was all she said, recognizing the edge of her own hunger, hearing the echo in his voice.

"It's getting easier to trust you." Neill backed out of the car, keeping her face in sight. "Now you know I don't trust myself. We'll have to keep moving until you want to stand still. Do you understand me?"

"Oh, yes," she managed to murmur, but her mouth was terribly dry.

"And you think I'm the one who's on the run." He stood on the corner, tall, immobile, as she drove away.

"I need a companion for this," laughed Neill on the other end of the phone. "Wear all your diamonds and a tiara, too. Her Honor, the mayor, will be there and several hundred others pretending to be Irish for one night."

Joyce tried to shield the mouthpiece of her receiver and keep the words in the cup of her hands. Brian Wiggins had a set of ears every bit as sharp as his twelve-year-old brain. "I can't. Really, the answer is no. I'm supposed to fly to St. Louis for the annual convention of childhood psychologists that evening. They don't care if it's St. Patrick's Day or not."

His voice grew slightly sly. "Are you going to discuss *me* at this meeting? Deliver your paper on me?"

"Not this year," Joyce retorted. "I need more facts and less fancy from you, I think. You must be feeling much better if you're worried about what kind of press you're going to get."

"I'm not worried and I am feeling much better, even able-bodied. I'm willing to give you facts galore and a fine night on the town to boot. Now, what time shall I call for you?"

Brian's eyes never once left hers. Joyce could almost see his pink ears wiggle, straining to hear. *Able-bodied*, she thought with a twinge of excitement and a visual flash of Neill, sprawled in sleep and naked in his sickbed. Able-bodied was both a fact and a force to be reckoned with.

"No," she said. "I mean, no time. I can't go. I'll speak to you later, Mr. Riordan. I have a client waiting."

"You have more than that waiting, Dr. Lanier," he said softly before she hung up.

"Tell me what's been happening in school this week," Joyce said to Brian, appalled at the unsteady and husky quality of her own voice.

Accepting Neill's invitation to the Palmer House for the city's biggest and most lavish celebration would be a date. There would be no way to pretend it was in the line of research or duty or anything remotely official. It was a social, public and highly publicized event. It would be a date.

A date meant she accepted the too-personal trend of their relationship. She would be encouraging those male-female aspects, in fact. She wasn't going to go.

The phone rang inside the apartment as Joyce was fumbling outside with her keys. She grabbed the receiver on the tenth ring.

"Seven o'clock," chimed Neill's voice. "It may be later if I can't remember how to do a damned bow tie."

"What? What?" Joyce shouted into the phone but the line was dead. "No," she said to thin air.

She heard the ringing as she was turning on the shower later. It was her own fault for not switching on the recording, on which a sweet-voiced, unperturbed Joyce said she was sorry but she couldn't come to the phone and please leave a brief message after the tone.

"This better be an emergency," Joyce said, clad in goose-pimpled splendor. "If this is you, Neill, it better be terminal."

"It may be," his rich baritone confirmed. "I've tied my silly cravat and it resembles a hangman's noose. Can you do better? I'm down here in your lobby."

"All I would do is tighten it until those wicked eyes bulge, Neill. In ten seconds, I'm going to be in the shower."

"Oh, we'll be fashionably late, then," Neill said evenly. "Don't fuss, love. You'll be fine whatever you're wearing."

Joyce looked down at her naked, slender body and laughed. "Only if I can go as a peeled stick." She hung up before he could comment on her lack of wardrobe or make her laugh again and shake her resolution.

The distance she wanted and needed from Neill was shrinking every time she saw him. She faced it and it was scary. When Neill looked at her a certain way, the question she was asking almost melted away. She wasn't the type who went weak-kneed, but he had an unsteadying effect on her stride. It would be so easy to tell him that she wanted him. She could let the smoldering tension between them flare up into a blaze of desire, burn her in a casual affair and be ashes before the year was over. She believed every word he'd told her but three. *I love you.*

The doorbell rang and rang until it sounded like an enraged insect. She knew who it was before she opened the door with the chain on. She was swathed in huge bath towels and her feet left wet prints on the tile.

"Not ready yet, eh?" Neill said cheerfully. "I'll wait here in the hall and entertain your neighbors until you're dressed." He thrust a bunch of green carnations through the narrow opening and began to pace up and down the carpet, bellowing "When Irish Eyes Are Smiling."

"That song requires a tenor," Joyce sneered, slamming the door closed. She laughed through "Danny Boy", endured "I'll Take You Home Again, Kathleen" and three others. She was dried, dressed and wrapped from throat to ankles in her black velvet cloak before Neill butchered "The Rising of the Moon".

"I'm going to regret this," she said, pushing him ahead of her to the elevator. "I don't want to get evicted, but this is musical blackmail."

The door to the left of hers swung open. "That was lovely," a disembodied voice said. "Do you know..."

Neill looked so smug, Joyce wanted to step on his patent dress shoes, but once she started to laugh, she couldn't stop. Neill insisted on a taxi, not her car. The cabbie thought she was the demented one, tying Neill's bow tie and howling.

"There are forty-three million descendants of the Irish in the United States," Neill informed her solemnly. "We must do some things right."

"Have babies?" guessed the driver while Joyce giggled helplessly. "Emigrate?"

"Not sing," she suggested as the cab arrived at the Palmer House. Neill was busy patting himself in the strange fashion she had come to recognize. "And not pay their own way. Staple your wallet to your leg, Neill, next time." She paid the fare, still amused.

It was hard for her to stay angry at him, she decided. There was no meanness or cruelty to Neill she could detect. He never apologized for any of his eccentricities or outrageous opinions, but she was used to working with steppers to very different drums.

Joyce checked her own coat; Neill had been accosted by a gray-faced man with a green top hat before they sailed through the gold and white lobby. She amused herself by spotting all the political bigwigs and society faces she could. It would surprise her if Neill felt any more at home in this company, with the glitter of chandeliers and the brittle sound of cocktail glasses clinking, than she did. Neill was a lot of things she couldn't label yet, but he wasn't a phony.

"I should have risked eviction," she whispered to him. "I can't believe you sang me into this."

"I was hoping to impress you," Neill growled, shoving her toward the ballroom. He sounded sincere. "I'd rather be hung, drawn and quartered than go to faculty teas or affairs of state."

She was stunned. "Impress me? Why on earth would you want to..."

"Why on earth would you want to wear orange?" Neill asked out of the corner of his mouth. The reception line inched forward and the couple ahead of them chatted amiably with the mayor, her husband and the other dignitaries.

"It's not orange. It's a deep peach," defended Joyce, glancing down at the sleek lines of her only long dress. "I have a kelly-green bathrobe. We could whip back to my apartment and I can throw it on over this for the dinner."

He grinned unexpectedly at her. "A green bathrobe? I must see it soon."

"Fat chance," Joyce murmured just as the rather portly Irish ambassador's wife grabbed her right hand in a death grip. The matron flushed and looked annoyed. Joyce felt a small wave of warmth herself and stammered something vague and conciliatory and awful like "Not you," as Neill chuckled in her left ear.

"I usually avoid these society gatherings like the plague," Neill said, grabbing another drink off the passing tray. "The Irish consul made it sound like a command performance, and I gave in."

"So did I," muttered Joyce, more to herself than to him. She made up her mind to make the best of the evening and somehow extract information about Neill's social habits in general. "Well, you seem to know lots of people here, there and everywhere. For a man who doesn't like to give interviews, you are pretty open and extroverted in other settings. Why do you think that is?"

"I'm not here giving interviews," Neill said, raising an eyebrow in warning. "And please, remember that! Now, try to look as though I didn't drag you here by the hair and we'll mingle with the great and near-great."

"Which category are you in?" Joyce asked peevishly.

His eyes turned slate-dark and flashed with mischief. "Great!"

His confidence nettled her almost as much as his appearance had unsettled her. She hadn't imagined how handsome and distinguished he would look in a tuxedo. It was one thing to know a man was attractive when he didn't seem to pay much attention to his looks. Tonight, she couldn't help wondering if he knew what effect he had on women—the reason so many female guests stood a little too close or touched his arm while they made inane conversation.

Joyce wandered away from him while a titian-haired Amazon was still gushing. After his newest admirer had asked Joyce, "Doesn't Erin produce the finest men...and the sexiest?" she'd shrugged to show her indifference or ignorance and fled.

After a few minutes, she peeked over the shoulder of the man lecturing her and spotted Neill. He had his hands full but it was not with the redhead. His forehead was creased and both he and his male companion were gesturing wildly at each other. She watched until her curiosity overcame her caution. She hadn't studied the famous Riordan temper up close, and Neill was very clearly in an argument.

"...have a duty to your people and homeland," the other man was saying as Joyce wove her way near them.

"I'll decide what that duty is," Neill retorted. "And it's not riding on a float, Mick. I've got a pen, not a flag or a gun—" He broke off abruptly when he saw Joyce at his elbow and grabbed her arm, pulling her slightly forward. "Dr. Joyce Lanier, Michael Boyle of Ireland United."

Joyce extended her hand and managed to keep her face calm and composed. Boyle switched topics to the parade down State Street and was civil. Before he excused himself, though, he gave Neill a hard, hooded stare and muttered a cryptic message about keeping tabs on who could be counted on.

"Michael Boyle," said Joyce in disbelief. "Neill, I've read enough about him and his group to know how militant they are. Of all people, I wouldn't expect you to have much to do with them. Your poetry's anti-war, anti-violence.... I *did* read your books and you're worlds apart from their philosophy."

"He's a transplanted Irishman, just like me," Neill said, and changed the subject immediately. "They're starting to seat people for the dinner. Shall we?"

"What does that mean? 'Just like me?' Are you active politically with any Irish-American groups? Joyce saw the muscles in his jaw twitch and felt his fingers tighten around her bare arm. She knew she was irritating him with the questions but she couldn't dismiss them now that she'd viewed another side of his complex personality.

"I don't like to talk politics. I don't like to talk religion," Neill rasped. "That rule applies to nosy reporters, scruffy expatriates, drinking buddies and even to beautiful psychologists."

She chose to ignore the compliment and the warm strength of his grip on her. "I don't know why I ever agreed to come here with you," she snapped. "And I don't know why you agreed, even in principle, to let me do a study on you, Riordan. You won't cooperate; you talk about what you want and refuse to answer questions I need to ask; we still meet in totally inappropriate places and at the weirdest times."

She stopped in her tracks at the table. The other couples were already seated and very interested in watching their unknown companions face off. Joyce was nearly past the point of caring. The color on her cheeks was not all blusher and the blue of her eyes deepened to a flashing sapphire.

"You're sure you're not Irish?" Neill asked. He pulled out her chair with a flourish, but Joyce refused to sit down. "You have the fire, that's sure, when you're not too busy playing the doctor."

"I *am* a doctor," exclaimed Joyce vehemently. She glanced around and noticed they were the last two people standing in the huge room. Sitting down quickly, she lowered her voice and glared at Neill. "You are my subject, I am the researcher. Why are we always fighting each other?"

"Because you are a woman and I am a man," Neill suggested with a smile and nod at the mesmerized couple across the table. "Because you are used to talking with little children with big minds."

"And now I have to deal with a big child with a little mind?" snipped Joyce. The clapping that greeted the introduction of the opening speaker made her break off any further conversation. After a minute or two, she was grateful for the drone of the remarks.

Damn the man, she thought, sneaking a sidelong glance at Neill. He deserved his stubborn reputation, but she could not ever remember a time in her career when she had lost her professional cool so completely, so easily. No one talked freely to her who didn't feel safe and secure from criticism.

"I'm sorry," she hissed at him when there was a lull. "I'm just on edge, I guess, because we haven't accomplished as much as I would have liked to."

"It's not from lack of trying," Neill shot back softly. He picked up her hand and put a kiss into the center of her palm. The tip of his tongue licked a tiny, damp spot on the soft, fragrant skin there. When she pulled her hand back, he gave her a lazy, wicked smile. "I haven't accomplished what I wanted, either."

The heat that flooded down her arm was so intense, Joyce wondered if she had turned the same color as her dress. Her anger changed without warning into an excitement running through her veins. She could not look away from him and she was sure Neill could see how his intimate gesture had affected her.

He was very much a man. He made her feel more like a woman than she had in a very long time. Joyce buttered a roll and nibbled at it, giving her hands an excuse to move, her mouth something to occupy itself with. The weekend ahead was starting to look better and better. She needed the chance to think about what was happening to her.

The dinner was served and Joyce pushed the food around on her plate with disinterest. She hardly heard a word of the interminable speeches from the dais. Thankfully, the others at the table were busy listening and eating, sparing her the ordeal of polite chitchat. Neill said nothing more, but he looked at her from time to time, and there was an obvious message in his glance.

He was bored and wanted to leave.

"I hate these," grumbled Neill midway into the third speech. "Everyone here is dressed up, drunk and dying to pick a fight."

"Then why did you agree to come?" Joyce repeated. "And why were you so set on dragging me along?" She realized their tablemates were far more interested in them than in the speaker or the corned beef. Her forced smile probably looked as pained as it felt.

"I thought you would cheer me up with your company." Neill took a large swallow of his green-tinted drink and shuddered. "Misery loves company."

"Misery insisted on company," Joyce retorted. "I suppose I can take notes on my napkin pertaining to your lack of social graces...or we can leave after this windbag gets through extolling—"

"Shut up, blondie. That's my brother," snarled the man across from Joyce. His jowls and neck had turned pinker than the corned beef.

"I beg your..." Joyce began, caught awkwardly between social grace and the truth.

Neill stood up slowly, resting his hand on her shoulder. "Don't beg unless you need bread," Neill cautioned her in a low, soft tone. "It's not my friend's fault or mine he's your brother and a windbag," he said to the now-scarlet diner, who was rising to his feet and the occasion. "Is it time for the dancing or did you have something else in mind, mister?"

"Neill!" Joyce struggled upward at his gentle restraint. The applause greeting the end of the boring program almost covered up her loud protest.

"I'm a precinct captain," announced the irate man as if his political job were a steel-edged weapon. He began to step around the table, jabbing the air in front of him with a menacing forefinger. "If you think—"

"I do think," snarled Neill, pushing Joyce rather gently out of his way. "I think you have fewer manners than I do, no sense of humor and if you don't sit down, I think you may lose more than this lady's vote."

She had never seen the famous Riordan temper before, but it was as real as rumored. Neill's eyes were absolutely blazing, and his wonderful, resonant voice had changed into a menacing, hard rumble. The strangest thing, Joyce realized, was her own weird mixture of feelings. Horror, of course, but also a bit of amusement and a strange, almost heady excitement. She'd never looked to a man to defend her before and had never expected such a response. But Neill was outraged, genuinely angry on her behalf.

"I think we should go," Joyce said weakly.

"You shouldn't have showed up in the first place," thundered the precinct captain. "I know all about you, Riordan. You artsy-craftsy types live to make trouble and get your picture in the paper. And these little society dames, looking down their noses..." He was gesturing expansively and flinging his arms too wide. His left hand hit Joyce's shoulder with a solid thump more by accident than design.

Joyce ignored the blow. It didn't hurt, and it didn't matter. All she could see was Neill's face gathering into a dark scowl like a thundercloud ready to rain, and his big hands gathering into fists. She wondered fleetingly who was going to bail them out of jail when the St. Patrick's Eve dinner dissolved into a classic donnybrook.

A flashbulb popped nearby, startling her into action. The precinct captain was almost within striking distance of Neill, his wife shrieking shrill encouragement, and a crowd of delighted onlookers was assembling.

Joyce put one hand on Neill's shirtfront, although she realized she couldn't hold him back any more than she could stop a train. "That's enough," she shouted, seeing Neill's hands slowly coming up. "This is not the Billy Goat Tavern, gentlemen."

The politician's wife knocked her chair back and almost tipped the table over in her haste to join the fun. One of the corned beef platters hit the shiny parquet floor and shattered, splattering Joyce with a fringe of cabbage. "Stay out of it, blondie," she hollered at Joyce.

"Great advice but too late," muttered Joyce under her breath. Why in the world had she managed to get herself linked up with the wandering minstrel of Erin in a public scene? Wouldn't Dr. Kyler have a few choice words for her on Monday?

She saw the precinct captain's feeble attempt to swing at Neill and, reaching out, gave the man a push backward.

To her utter amazement, the man took a tiny step back to regain his balance, bumped against a serving cart and slipped down to the floor in a graceless heap. It was like watching a big balloon collapse. Three flashbulbs went off and captured the scene in a bright silver and purple flare.

The precinct captain was sitting there waving his arms ineffectually, unable to close the small surprised circle of his mouth.

"Well done," said Neill loudly with a little laugh. "You can certainly take care of yourself, Joyce, but are you any good at arm wrestling?"

His face was lit with delight, all his anger sizzled as quickly as the incident itself. His eyes sparkled with a secret mischief, and Neill took her arm and pushed her ahead of him through the thin circle of whispering, giggling guests.

"How awful!" Joyce stopped outside the ballroom and rested for a minute against the wall. She put her ice cold hand up to her face and felt the incredible heat of her cheeks. "Oh, Neill, how could you?"

"How could I *what*?" He grinned disarmingly and stepped in front of her, blocking her view of the lobby. "I didn't start it, my dear, and I didn't even get a chance to finish it. It was the highlight of the whole evening, believe me. I'll *always* remember that fine expression on the fellow's face as he sat in the crockery and the carrots." He broke off, laughing loudly.

"Ohhhhh," moaned Joyce miserably. Every encounter with Neill was like a roller-coaster ride with unpredictable ups and downs. She was getting more insight into her own conventionality than into his genius. *"This* isn't going to work, Neill."

"It's working nicely," he countered without having to ask what "it" was. "We're a terrific tag team."

"I'm a psychologist, a professional..." wailed Joyce. "I'm a..."

His mouth was on hers and she was quickly reminded that she was a woman, too.

Five

Her own reaction shocked her as much as the sudden reunion of his mouth with hers. The Palmer House simply vanished, noise, potted palms and all, and dissolved into the thrilling pleasure of his kiss. Neill's lips moved on hers with slow, searching deliberation and she responded with silent questions of her own.

God, he tasted good. He felt good. Her reluctance to be here tonight and tempt fate had dissolved with a single kiss. All her weeks of hard work, the hours of proper and polite conversation, were toppling with the hot pressure of his mouth and the gentle stroke of his hands over her shoulders and back. Nothing he had told her was as exciting as the quick thrust and retreat of his tongue. Nothing was as rewarding as the sway of their bodies toward each other and the small, wordless cry rising in her throat.

She felt the trembling start and knew he could feel it, too. It was an admission that she was waiting, expectant. The tiny current of tension snaking through her limbs wanted to grow, to spread and explode.

Neill's mouth rose reluctantly from hers. He said her name as if he were as astonished as she was by what had happened. The lights and shadows and sounds surrounding them slowly reassembled into a reality. Her light-headedness and the turning, whirling sensation faded, but the tight, tingling feelings seemed permanently locked inside her.

"I'm going home," Joyce said shakily.

She wanted Neill to stop studying her and say something. Anything. She was fine when they were talking. She had survived the whole bizarre evening so far to find herself trapped by an embrace that passed unnoticed by the crowd of revelers.

She went to claim her coat with Neill dogging her steps. He hadn't said a word and his silence infuriated her. He didn't offer to help her into the folds of the midnight velvet cloak, and the absence of his touch was a relief. The air around them seemed to be electric, still vibrating, and she was the one who wanted to run, to keep moving, before the storm broke.

The cab ride to the Palmer House had been short and filled with giddy, silly laughter. The ride back was interminable and quiet. What was Neill waiting for? An invitation to spend the night? An admission that she was wrong about her ability to juggle her job and her feelings?

"My plane's very early tomorrow," Joyce said at her door. "I'm not going to ask you in, Neill."

"I didn't ask to come in. That's not what I want from you...now."

The last word registered. *Don't ask*, warned the humming warmth of her blood. Her fingers loosened their grip on the doorknob and left the keys dangling in the lock. *Don't ask what he wants.*

"You're a swan poised for flight," he said very softly. His hand slipped into the coat sleeve, brushing upward as lightly as humanly possible. "You've never really flown before, never soared with love. I saw it tonight in your eyes. It's happening to you. I only want to hear you say it."

Each feathery touch telegraphed itself to other, less accessible places. The skin on her stomach, the backs of her knees, her hardened nipples safely hidden under chiffon and lace, reacted as if he were stroking her all over.

"Say what? That I'm a woman, first, foremost and always? Okay, I am. That the chemistry between us is very strong? Yes." She had to take little gulps of air between phrases.

His other hand slipped through the cloak and encircled her waist before his fingers found a slow, circular pattern to follow along her sides. "You're looking at me as a man—only as a man—right now. Say you want me. You want me as much as I want you."

"No! Don't—don't do this," Joyce answered weakly. His insistence on the truth meant the end of the study, the end of what she was comfortable with. Around and around, his fingers kept moving, lost in the thin folds of her dress. "Adults can't have everything they want. I understand that. Why can't you? I can't be childish and irresponsible with you."

"Why not?" Neill demanded. "You wanted to touch the heart of genius, and you have." He seized her hand and brought it to his chest. Under the satiny lapels and starched white shirt, the rapid slamming of his heart matched her own.

"You want to find the source of genius, the inspiration, the pain..." His hand shifted hers downward. "I want to hear you say you want me—skin, bones, muscles, even this...."

Her captive hand felt the heated swell of his manhood and all thought of comfort and safety burned away. She was powerless to seek the easy way out and lie.

"I want you," Joyce whispered self-consciously. The simple truth was a hundred times harder to say aloud than she had imagined.

Neill didn't look triumphant. His eyes locked with hers, probing so deeply, she had the sense that he was trying to see right through her. "How sweet that sounds after all my waiting, all your pretending," he said. "Patience is a virtue. It happens not to be one of mine, but you can teach me, I'm sure. You're excessively, obsessively patient."

There was the throbbing of power and need in her palm but only tenderness and even a faint note of resignation in his voice. He took her hand gently away from himself and held her for a few minutes without kissing or caressing her, without another word.

Joyce stood very still in the circle of his arms, hearing the flutter of their breathing and the echo of her own admission. Wanting him was fine as long as she could mask it under the guise of friendship. Wanting him openly changed all her plans, threw away her chances to work with him. Without force or promise or commitment, Neill had wrested the truth from her and she had slammed the door closed on her own ambition.

"You've worn me down. You've worn me out," Joyce murmured, closing her eyes and letting her forehead rest on his chest. "In the war of personalities, Neill, you are the stronger and there's nothing I can teach you. You don't play by the rules."

"There are no rules," Neill answered. "In love, in poetry, there are no rules because it's not a game."

He cradled her head and tipped it back, his casual strength awing her, but he could not force her to open her eyes. She tried to turn sideways, but it was impossible. In his hands she felt frail, breakable. The forbidden, unwanted thought that she was already halfway in love with him peeked out of some remote, dark corner of her mind and if she opened her lids, she might see it reflected in the silvery mirrors of Neill's eyes. She wanted him. She was afraid of him.

"A bird without flight. A diamond without sparkle. You have everything fine and good but the daring that love takes," Neill insisted. "I have it in abundance, darling, and I'll give it gladly to you. I'll teach you recklessness and daring if you'll love me."

"That's enough, Neill. Stop this crazy talk." She felt tears well up under her shuttered eyelids. What gifts, she thought bitterly. What terrible gifts his foolhardiness, his endless headlong rushing around, his devil-may-care daring would be. "You're not my professor; I'm not your teacher. Our education's ended tonight. I'll want you but I won't love you."

Her blur of tears made it safe to look at him. She could only distance herself from him if she couldn't see him, now or ever. The prospect hurt but the pain, she knew, would fade. He was a disturbing presence to be cast out of her life before she did or said more she would regret.

"The longer you cling to dullness, the less chance you have to shine," Neill said. His lips brushed over the salty moisture at the corners of her eyes and then he stepped back, letting her go. "I'll be here when you get back, and when you are ready to cling to me, you tell me. I can wait."

He was gone before Joyce completely absorbed the message. With those long, purposeful strides she found so difficult to keep up with, Neill pivoted and disappeared around the bend in the corridor.

The effort to get undressed drained every bit of her remaining strength. Joyce sat on the couch, contemplating her suitcase and massaging her aching temples with numbed fingers. Sleep was out of the question. She fumbled in the drawer of the end table for her journal.

Her intention to record a brief ending to three months was no firmer than her handwriting. Exorcising her demons was difficult when every line called up a lunatic jumble of images and emotions: a dinner where the only food she remembered was on the floor, a porky politician and an irate Irishman, Neill singing in her hall. Her hand shook.

If she wrote it all out, she could close the book on Neill Riordan. There would be no need to read this entry full of senseless laughter and tears, arguments and embraces. Poetic license did not mean he could say and do whatever he wanted—she was no bird, no diamond, and not his love. He was crazy and she was sane. Joyce scratched out *cling to dullness* so vigorously, her pen ripped the paper.

The next page was blank, a clean and pristine tomorrow. Joyce closed the journal and put it away. "I want you," she said experimentally, unable to believe she had spoken those words. He was gone; it was safe to say them.

"I want you," Joyce repeated miserably and the words evaporated in the emptiness of the living room. She watched the sky turn to pearl and gray, the colors of a pair of eyes she was fleeing, and she hoped for a change in the weather—blue skies to St. Louis—and a change in the truth.

It was inevitable. Neill had said they were fated to be friends and lovers, but Joyce wasn't a believer in fate. Hadn't she always picked and chosen the events that shaped her life, the options open to her? *Yes, of course, I have*, she decided, trying to push last night from her mind. Neill just hadn't understood the whole point to her explanations of herself.

She didn't get swept off her feet by men. She didn't act impulsively in her work or in her life. There was nothing secret or mysterious or tragic about her, by design. Neill's intimation that all her planning and practicality sounded dull shouldn't sting quite as much as it still did.

"Do you think I'm dull?" she asked Julia on the way to O'Hare airport.

Julia hesitated long enough to lose her place in her tirade about Frank. "No, you're very, very bright. Why? Did you argue with Dr. Kyler about the handling of one of your kidlets again?"

"Nothing like that," Joyce said quickly. "Kyler and I don't agree on many things except to disagree. No, me, my insistence on a quiet, organized life—does that strike you as dull?"

"How it strikes me isn't important, is it?" asked Julia with more insight than her sister gave her credit for. "You're happy at the Bennett. You're always busy talking about how great your work is, how rewarding. I think your life is boring but you...well, you are more *even*."

Joyce liked the sound of the word. It gave her a mental image of herself as a road, straight and direct. There weren't steep hills or unexpected, stomach-twitching dips. There weren't detours and blind curves and dead ends to her. She was even. The image kept flashing through her mind during the flight to St. Louis, reinforced by the glimpses of narrow threads of road beneath them. She was a nice, even road and she had crossed somewhere along the way with Neill Riordan, a man like a twisting, rutted, dangerous mountain pass.

She liked playing with the metaphor and expanding on it. It would be something Neill could grasp and appreciate.

It was too late to tell him her literary inspiration. While she registered at the hotel and plastered on her name tag, Joyce was drawing a mental map of two roads meeting and spreading across the landscape.

"Lanier!" shouted a voice across the lobby. "Joyce, over here!"

"Alan," she called back, working her way through the knots of colleagues. It was going to be good to see old friends and classmates here, even old boyfriends. Neill Riordan only thought he'd invented love and romance, Joyce thought with a touch of smugness.

"Great to see you," Alan shouted a split-second before Joyce got a very big, very wet kiss. He didn't relinquish his hold on her one second all the way to the hotel bar, and before the first drink was downed, Joyce had figured out why. Alan was in the marriage market again, and Joyce had once been his first choice.

"...devastated by the divorce." He sighed and gave Joyce a soulful look. "It would have been better if I'd stayed in the Windy City to build my practice...and my life."

Joyce reminded him gently that he was here as one of the honored speakers. His practice couldn't be in much better shape. She wouldn't rise to the bait. She couldn't.

"And your work? What's new, Joyce?"

She heard herself talking about the clinic and her project with Neill. It sounded clinical and dull, but Alan was suitably impressed. Alan was, she remembered, very impressed with famous people, with getting ahead, with making a name for himself.

"What a break for you," he interrupted. "The guy was always being mentioned in New York when he was there. Supposed to get the Nobel Prize, sooner or later. Your paper will win you points."

She thought about bringing a future Nobel laureate a Snoopy coloring book, and smiled. She thought about sleeping in Neill's arms, and a visible shiver went through her.

"This calls for another drink," Alan declared. He signaled the waiter and reached for Joyce's hand. "Three years since we've gotten together, but as Freud said, separation brings about real growth."

Joyce looked up from her intense study of ice cubes and nodded agreement. She gently took her hand from under his. A heaviness she couldn't identify had formed in her chest and made breathing difficult.

"He's moody and intense," she said carefully. Her fingers flexed, remembering the texture of Neill's skin.

"Who? Oh, Riordan," Alan grunted. "Unpredictable, disorganized, not academic but brilliant and not stuffy. I've read it and I'm sure you've treated the type before."

Stop it, she thought, but she kept visualizing Neill jumping up and down on a crowded street corner in perfect rhythm with the Don't Walk sign. The weight in her grew. "Neill is not a type. He is unique."

Alan stared at her morosely. "How nice!"

"He's not *nice*," Joyce said before she could bite back the words. "Sometimes he's kind and tender but hardly nice."

Alan was nice. Alan was the personification of all the nice men she had ever dated, and she had refused to marry Alan, to everyone's horror. But Alan's voice didn't run through her like a mild electric shock, and Neill's did. Neill's mouth and hands did things to her which were anything but nice.

"I was referring to your opportunity to get at Neill Riordan," snorted Alan. He was trying to catch the waiter's eye and was openly miffed by Joyce's inattentiveness.

"I think Neill Riordan's gotten to me," sighed Joyce. Separation might bring about growth and it might bring out a longing she wasn't eager to acknowledge. "Sorry, Alan."

"For what?" he asked gruffly, throwing a few bills on the table. "You always were too preoccupied with your work, Joyce. Nothing's changed, obviously."

She didn't argue with his assessment.

Preoccupied with graduate school, she had chosen Alan as the man most likely. They shared their struggle for a doctorate, the search for a career in the same field, and, briefly, plans for a future together. She had picked a nice man for a perfect marriage. The Laniers were all giddy with delight at her good fortune, her mature and intelligent decisions.

It was as romantic as the merger of two corporations, thought Joyce viciously. When Alan took the best offer, it meant relocation to New York, and she wasn't willing to give up her little piece of pie at the Bennett for a bite at the Big Apple. They talked out their feelings very maturely, very intelligently, and talked themselves right out of each other's lives without harsh words or tears or regrets.

When someone asked her at the opening session where she was from, Joyce said, "Dullsville" and meant it. She told Riordan anecdotes at the banquet and hated herself for it. What she felt for Neill was no laughing matter and the polite, interested amusement of her colleagues only added to the burden her heart was carrying.

She almost gave in and picked up the phone. There would be his voice to hold on to but it wouldn't do. His brogue was broad but not as broad as his shoulders, not as warm as he was when she held him, not as sweet as he was to be with. She was waiting for another head-on collision with him, not a long-distance call.

There was no doubt that Neill was a rare breed of man as well as a great poet. He was on his way to fame, although his literary honors wouldn't make him a fortune. Unless she was reading him all wrong, even the Nobel Prize, if and when he won it, would make no basic changes in Neill's lifestyle.

He had never owned a house, a car, or more clothes than he could carry over one arm—or wanted to. Without the taint of antisocial feeling, he was a genuine nonconformist, liking people but not particularly giving a hoot what anyone thought of him.

She thought of him constantly. The whole weekend was one big marathon think, a solo brainstorming session. For years, no one had strummed emotional chords in her she couldn't identify and once a feeling was labeled, Joyce was perfectly capable of dealing with it.

But what could she call what Neill did to her? He made her laugh and cry and want to sink through the floor of a hotel ballroom. She lost her temper with him and fibbed to protect herself. From what? It was clear he didn't have to force women or men or children to achieve his ends; a smile usually sufficed.

Not with me, Joyce thought, conjuring up his face. Telling Neill she wanted him was candor, not surrender. The Irish rebels' motto, "No Surrender" was hers, too.

She needed to meet an intelligent, sane and settled man, someone who had mapped out his future as carefully as she had hers. The bald fact that years of dating such men, including Alan, had been like living in the desert, hoping the oasis would appear. It was discouraging when Neill, who was marginally sane, incurably unstable and constitutionally incapable of commitment, made her crazy with just a smile.

She wished she had more faith in mental telepathy. He'd be there at O'Hare. She wished she believed in magic. She had the feeling she was going to be sawn in half. The magician was ready to vanish into thin air and it wasn't a trick. Oh, God, Joyce thought, it was love.

Six

The jet sighed heavily back onto the runway at O'Hare in a light rain. By the time Joyce made her way through the crowd of passéngers, coming and going, the rain was pouring down. Long silvery slashes of water hit the wide terminal windows with an angry sound. There would not be a free cab in weather like this. She shifted her coat, draped over her arm, trying to decide her next move. Telephone Julia and Frank? Then she heard her own name at almost the exact instant Neill's face appeared across the mobbed corridor.

The flight had been smooth. Now, suddenly, she felt a lurching. A pinpoint of heat centered itself in her chest. "Neill, how strange... I wasn't expecting you to pick me up." She smiled, but there was no broad grin in return.

"I had to see you," Neill said somberly. "It was a long and rough three days."

"Well, a welcoming committee is supposed to look happy."

He didn't respond until Joyce got closer. Putting his arms around her, Neill pulled her close. His tan trench coat was patched with darker brown. The cold and damp against the front of Joyce's blouse went right through her, but his eyes looked incredibly warm.

"I missed you about three months' worth these last few days," he said very softly. His lips brushed hers in the ritual public kiss of travelers, but Joyce shivered.

It wasn't the clammy, wet feeling of his coat or even his look and embrace that made her tremble. Something wild and heated flared deep inside her when he said exactly what she was thinking. She had longed for him, thought about him all the time she was in St. Louis, without wanting to admit it or put a name on the feeling.

"I missed you, too," she admitted slowly. "I almost called Saturday night just to hear your brogue and tell you—" she stopped herself in time by glancing away from the stormy question building in his eyes. It had almost slipped out. *I think I'm in love with you* "—how boring a conference can be after an adventure at the Palmer House with you. Shall I tell you how dull it was? I learned nothing except that a cup of coffee in a hotel can cost over a dollar."

"No, don't tell me about it now." He tilted his face slightly and a very faint smile curved the ends of his mouth. "You're the one whose job it is to listen and I have all sorts of things I want to talk about."

He kept one arm around her shoulders as they headed toward the baggage claim. Joyce liked the feeling it gave her. The pressure of his arm almost dissolved the hidden weight she'd been carrying around inside her for days. But she didn't like the slight note of urgency or mystery in his voice.

"Neill, is something wrong?" His slowness to reply and his sober expression in profile worried her. "What is it?"

They stopped at the slowly revolving luggage carousel and studied the suitcases in silence for a few minutes.

"You shouldn't have come out in this weather. You still look dragged out from the flu, or you're upset. What's wrong?"

Finally, he answered and reached for the plaid suitcase she was pointing out. "Perhaps nothing. Perhaps everything's actually right...missing you, coming here to take you home, everything. I had to find out."

"What? What's going on?" She hurried along, losing ground to his long strides as Neill led the way to a battered VW. From the ragged bumper stickers and window decals, Joyce guessed one of his students had made him the generous loan.

She found part of the answer on the seat of the car. Neill gestured at the folded newspaper dated the eighteenth of March. He concentrated on the eccentricities of the car's gears and Joyce scanned the well-worn page the paper fell open to. There was a grainy but recognizable photo in the feature on the St. Patrick's Day ball.

She was quiet until the surprise and shock passed. Her own startled face, Neill's beautifully captured scowl and the precinct captain's dismay as being floored deserved all her attention.

"'Poet Packs a Punch,'" she read aloud. "Oh, great, they got it all wrong. Even the spelling of my name. Try not to find every bump, Neill. The light's not very good in here, either."

"You know I didn't hit him," Neill said tersely.

"I'll bet Dr. Kyler at the clinic loved this," Joyce speculated. "The Bennett needs all the publicity it can get for fund-raising. Hell-raising, I'm not so sure about."

"I'm sorry," he said, glancing at her. "You probably want to take a swing at me. I'll call Kyler, if you like, and explain the whole mess to him."

Joyce chewed her bottom lip, slightly amazed at her own reaction. Somehow, she was not angry or embarrassed by the article and picture. She was more concerned because Neill obviously was so worried. *He cares*, she thought. *He really cares about me.* Strangely, inexplicably, she wanted to laugh.

"You're the celebrity, I'm not," she said, declaring his offer. "Any explanation will tarnish your hard-won reputation as the flamboyant, controversial poet. No one, even Kyler, will believe I decked the guy, and I don't think they'll fire me for bar-brawling. Do you?"

The laughter would not be kept down. She started to giggle and it erupted into a full-throated sound. Neill shook his head in disbelief and then joined in. "No, but I didn't expect you to take it so well," he chuckled. "I thought you might roll up the paper and smack me with it. You are a rather go-by-the-rules lady, you know, and here you end up linked with a literary oddball. You didn't want to go to that celebration of fools in the first place. You sure you're not mad?"

"Maybe mad as in crazy, but not angry," Joyce assured him. Folding the newspaper, she tucked it away in her canvas satchel as if it were a souvenir, then focused on the glow of the expressway lights. Being with him, knowing how she felt about him and not acting on it was crazy. It was going to get crazier if she didn't take some action.

"I didn't know insanity was contagious," Neill said, giving her the full benefit of one of his genuine smiles. His look moved over her quickly and it was a caress, full of promise. "We'll be a matched pair of fools, then, but I'll try not to drag you to rack and ruin with me. Maybe some of your sensible, conservative nature will infect me, Doctor."

"I doubt it," Joyce whispered inaudibly before she found the strength to look straight at him. "I had to give up my plan for the study on you, Neill. As the odd couple around town, we aren't getting much accomplished and—" she forced herself not to drop her voice "—I seem to have lost all objectivity when it comes to you."

"What a way with words you have," exclaimed Neill as he drove into the parking lot of her building. He maneuvered the VW into the first open space he spotted and turned off the engine. "You make love sound like an affliction, Joyce."

"This isn't my space. You can't park here," Joyce was saying before she realized what he had said.

"Neill, I didn't say anything about loving you," she protested even as he was reaching for her.

"I don't need the words." In the cold air his breath burned her cheek and then his lips hovered very close to her mouth. "I need you."

The simple declaration took away her ability to speak and his kiss stole any desire to talk. The soft pressure of his lips increased until Joyce met the sweet probe of his tongue. She returned the searching, sliding pleasure he was eager to give her, letting the mating of their mouths say more than she could have. She could feel sanity slipping away, drowning in the good taste of the man, the mingled scent of Neill and rain.

Her teeth nipped lightly at the fullness of his lower lip, teasing at the hunger she sensed in him, but the shock of wanting also ran through her. The groan he made and the soft sigh from Joyce made no sense in any language. The sounds joined and hung in the close confinement and were very telling.

"I didn't want to get involved with you," Joyce murmured when his kisses began to trail along the line of her jaw and seek a haven at her throat. "There are all these problems...."

"Mmmm," Neill hummed agreeably against the smoothness of her neck. His lips worked, damp, warm and unhurried, tasting her. "Little problems?"

One of his hands found its way into the open suit jacket and cupped her breast. His thumb brushed around and over the hardened nipple until the tingling became an ache. Joyce's mind struggled to recall the problems while her body clamored for more sensation as the only solution. Her fingers reached to touch his face gently and trace the curve of his ear. With more strength she stroked his springy, still-damp hair and cradled his head.

"No, big problems," she answered in a voice thickened with need and sadness. Wanting him, she had lost him for her study. And she would lose him when they were lovers. In months, he would be gone again. She would never be able to claim she had not seen the inevitable end of love from this night of new beginnings.

His lips still clung to her skin, but the kisses ended. His hand held her, but the wonderful stroke of his fingers stopped. Neill's head rose slowly and he drew back slightly. In the dim lighting of the parking area she could see little more than a glint from his eyes and the hard, almost stern lines of his face.

"But you love me," he said quietly, and there was no questioning to the statement this time. "You're always the one who talks about the difficulty of us meeting and working together in inappropriate places. You're right. A cramped VW is no place to explore problems or feelings."

When he reached over and tenderly brushed the loose strands of hair back from her cheek, Joyce knew what she wanted. More than an exploration of problems or feelings, she wanted the exploration of his hands, his mouth, his body. She wanted the discovery of him and if she waited too long, she would never know it. There might be only one year, one month or one night to share, but she wanted it with Neill. She clung to him.

"Let's go up to the apartment," she whispered.

He didn't move or say anything right away. There was a single sharp intake of breath and he kept staring at her for what seemed like hours. Finally, Neill touched his fingers very delicately to her mouth.

"I can't." He hesitated, then cleared his throat. "I can't unless I can make love to you, Joyce. Despite your job, I've been driven crazy by you, wanting you. I don't trust myself to go up there and be able to talk or even make sense. The only things I want to hear are the noises we would make giving and getting pleasure from each other, the echo of my satisfaction coming from your throat. Do you understand?"

"Perfectly," Joyce said hoarsely. She took out her key and pressed it into his hand. "Now, let's go upstairs. I couldn't have said it better myself, but I just don't have your way with words."

The tension broke in a flood, and Neill smiled, looking at the key as if she had performed a magic trick. The door on his side opened with a popping sound. Neill took the suitcase and put his free arm around Joyce's waist. They looked straight at the elevator door and not at each other. Neill shortened his stride to make it easier for Joyce to walk with him, but once they reached the steel door he forgot to maintain his pose of cool composure. He slapped impatiently at the hollow metal and gave Joyce a distinctly devilish, impatient look.

"Well, at least I didn't break into a run," he said, making her laugh all the way up to her floor.

The key turned smoothly in the lock and the laughter died. They were two shadows moving in the gloom of her apartment, the sweeping darkness of desire there also, like a tangible presence. Joyce did not reach automatically for the light tonight. This was not a night for light, logic or reason. Her passion for Neill had overruled the safety of the familiar. Without turning to him, she slipped off her shoes and shrugged the suit jacket from her shoulders. Only the sounds of his coat rustling and his breathing assured her Neill was there, waiting behind her.

He proclaimed himself an impatient man before she left for St. Louis, but he was not touching her, not rushing to wield the power he had shown her before. No, she was the one whose blood was singing a song of eagerness, chorused by the faster beat of her heart.

The words were there, the key to unlock the tension, and she suddenly said them. "I want you. I want all of you, Neill."

It was as if she had stumbled onto a magical incantation, a charm so strong it could not be overcome. His hands were on her shoulders, drawing Joyce back to allow his warmth to mingle with hers. "You have all of Neill Riordan already," he whispered, his lips moving on the back of her head, his fingers gentle. "You just didn't seem to know it before."

She would now. Before morning she would know more of him than she had allowed herself to dream of. The lingering doubts were being burnt away by the brush of his warm mouth on the back of her neck.

The years of caution dropped with the descent of his touch, freeing her blouse from the waistband and then trapping the firmness of flesh in his cupped hands. She moaned softly, feeling her breasts budding and the need for Neill blooming like a flower heavy with morning dew.

Her head was too heavy to support; she let it fall back to his chest. Whether Neill knew it or not, he was holding her up as she melted, molded to him. The light circling strokes of his thumb and forefinger around her nipples transformed them into aching, hard knots and sapped all strength from her arms and legs.

His fingers started tiny, unquenchable fires under her skin as they caressed the rounded undersides and stretched the fire into trails running down to her stomach. Every nerve ending clamored for more heat, but Joyce was silent, washed by a weakness she had never experienced before.

There were other ways to tell him how much she wanted him. Her hands dropped to cover his and guide them to the zipper on her skirt. Her hips slid from side to side in a gentle but deliberate motion. Neill was already taut with the same hunger, but he would not be hurried.

"I've waited so long for you," he said in a strained and throaty voice, "that now this waiting is pleasure." His tongue traced the curve of her ear as his fingers obligingly undid her skirt and pushed it down until it fell unheeded around her feet.

Her blouse followed, fluttering like a white moth in the darkness. Her body quivered in anticipation when his hand flattened on her stomach, working his fingers under the waistband of her panty hose to glide downward.

"Yes, touch me...kiss me," Joyce asked in a voice she scarcely recognized.

"I will, love. Everywhere," Neill promised softly. She arched into his touch when he discovered the heated, damp invitation she offered, and it frayed his self-control and made his breathing ragged. "But slowly, darling, slowly, or it will be over before we've begun."

It frightened him a little to hear himself confess the truth and admit how thin his hold on himself was. It was so easy to tell her things no other woman had ever heard. He wanted to give her everything of himself, perhaps far more than she wanted. There was more magic than he had suspected, and he wanted to make the night last forever.

His eyes hadn't looked their fill. Neill pivoted her in his arms and the sight of her pale pearl body, the half-clad slender length, the shifting of long legs, did nothing to cool his blood. Her white arms rose almost as gracefully as his imagined swan-daughter's wings and met around his neck.

Joyce said his name once, and his mouth dipped to stop her before she could croon him to haste. His tongue filled her with the same thrust, the same primitive, wild exaltation his hips longed to fill her with. He drank in the softness and the moist warmth of her as if his thirst would never be assuaged.

Then Joyce understood why they were still standing there, why there was no end or relief to the wild song in her heart. Neill had promised to teach her the daring that love takes and she felt the force of it now. Words were useless. There were better ways to speak to each other.

She took his hand and led him into the bedroom. It was strangely wonderful to stand naked before him and return favor for favor, undressing him. Now she could tease and linger over each button of his shirt, brush her fingers over him as she opened the buckle of his belt. Every sound Neill made, every sharp intake of his breath, was a tribute to boldness and to the sharing this night should be.

When all his clothes were shed, Joyce looked at him as he had looked at her. Lightly, her fingertips explored the length and breadth of his beauty, his mystery. She smiled at Neill with wonder and pleasure and his answer was a smile, the throb of savage need as her fingers closed around him.

She saw how much he wanted her and gloried in it. She risked more to carry them both to a new, higher level of need, sliding her hands over him, kissing him all over with growing abandon until nothing else existed but them.

Neill was less gentle now. He put her on the bed, joining her quickly, and the contact of skin to skin was electric.

"I'm ready," Joyce cried. Her nails bit into the rippling muscles of his back as if she could spur him.

"I'm not," muttered Neill, although each time he moved his body contradicted him.

Her lips parted, her eyelids began to close with the sure, steady progress of his mouth down her. His kisses, frenzied and hot, outlined the curve of her shoulders, the length of her torso, and nursed hungrily on the roundness of each breast. He did not want compliance or acceptance or even readiness; he wanted madness, and Joyce embraced it willingly.

She was sure she would go crazy if he lingered this long on the silkiness of her stomach, the soft hair at the joining of her thighs. Her knees parted and she moved helplessly to the steady urging of his probing fingers, his fevered kisses.

The rush of blood was a sea in her head, deafening her. His body slid up hers like a wave and Joyce cried out again, lifting her hips, reaching and guiding him and it was a demand too sweet to resist.

Neill sank heavily into her, pinning her with the hard force of his passion. He could not stop the driving rhythm of his hips, the frenzied slide deeper and deeper into the wet silk of her body.

But there was no more need for waiting or caution. Joyce was as lost in the delight and joy of him as he was in her. The arching of her back, the sting of her nails along his ribs and thighs, were more eloquent than words. The rocking of her body was an answer and a plea at once.

"Yes, everything...everything," Neill groaned, seeing the taut quiver of her flesh as he surged and retreated again and again. His hands slid under her, clutching and opening her for the pleasure he wanted more and more to give her.

He shuddered and ground his mouth on her to hold back the sounds, wonderful and meaningless and too exciting to hear, of impending satisfaction. Joyce whimpered and rose up and Neill felt the telltale tremors shake her, twist her, and he wouldn't stop moving, wanting every cell of her to acknowledge him, to know she was his.

"And more," he rasped in triumph.

Joyce could not believe there was more sensation possible. Her head turned slowly side to side, a dazed denial of what she was feeling. There was nothing in the universe but the yielding softness beneath her, his heated hardness above her and in her and the incredible, endless release that shook her to the core. She surrendered to him and gave herself wholly to the wonder. What was total possession was total freedom, and the fury of it shattered her.

There was triumph, too, when she heard Neill call her name. He stiffened and trembled in her arms, pushing and plunging in the final, deepest throes of his own release. Then he lay very still under the stroke of her slippery palms, very still in the grip of her binding leg.

They clung together for long, quiet minutes, too weak to move. When Neill's lips found hers now, it was with an infinite tenderness, a message that had no words in any language but is understood by all. Very slowly, he shifted himself next to her.

"Please don't sleep yet," he pleaded.

Joyce smiled, lazy and languorous, at him.

The silence in the room was almost total, a hushed peace within her. She was listening to the slowly ebbing tides subside and it took a long time for the music of passion to quiet. Next to her, Neill was still, but each time she opened her eyes, she saw him watching her, his head pillowed very close to hers, the pupils in his eyes wide in the dim light.

When he finally moved, it was to prop himself on one elbow and stare down intently at her. "Are you happy?" Neill asked hoarsely.

The expression on his face more than the question alerted Joyce. It was more than an idle query. Neill, doubtful? She had never picked up the slightest hint before that he lacked in self-confidence or assurance like any other man.

"I'm very happy," she whispered back. "You are the kind of lover women dream of but don't believe exist—patient and gentle, virile and satisfying." The last word came out in an involuntary purr.

Neill smiled almost shyly. "I was so eager and frightened all at once. I was afraid I wanted you too much to please you."

Joyce was thankful she was lying down, too spent with making love to react outwardly as she did inwardly. She never expected a lover like Neill Riordan, and she never expected the kind of trust and daring it took for a man—any man—to expose his fears and insecurities. His soft confession touched her as deeply as his hard body had and it fed a kind of courage in her as well.

"It wasn't like that before, Neill. Not for me, not ever. I thought...well, I guess I thought it's nice, it's okay, but it's not earthshaking. I told myself it's ordinary for ordinary people and then, this was..." Her voice trailed off when she saw the reflection of herself in the twin silver mirrors of Neill's eyes. She even looked different to herself: softer, glowing, beautiful.

"Perfect," Neill said, bringing her closer and tucking the sheet around them both. "You are perfect."

She chuckled sleepily. "A bit on the thin, flat-chested side. Tall, stringy blondes are a dime a dozen, Mr. Riordan."

"Cheap at twice the price, but I'm talking about you. You have no idea of how long a man out of place has to look for a woman out of time."

"You have no idea how many times I don't follow the things you say." Joyce rolled over to rest her chin on her hands and her hands on his chest. "I've got very educated ears, but you're a real challenge. 'Out of place, out of time.' Is it a new poem? A symbol, a metaphor? I might be out of touch." His slow, languid caresses along her spine proved Joyce wrong. His deep respiration reverberated through him right into her bones. "Belfast," Neill murmured, and his arms wreathed her, warm and real, but Joyce could almost see him drift away. "It's a place of strife now, as it was then. I was born there and, for a while, it was the place I prayed to escape. I did run, every chance I got, and along my roads, years later, I stumbled on the rutted truth in myself. It wasn't just Belfast I had to leave, love. It was every place I went. I didn't fit them or they, me. I worked in a coal mine, at the ship docks, in factory and farm. It wasn't the jobs and it wasn't the people in the towns that drove me out or on. It's me."

She didn't realize she was holding her breath until Neill took one and she followed suit, feeling faint. Wanderlust was a positive attribute when she compared it to what Neill was describing: a rootless, homeless, endless isolation. Clinging to the solid island of his torso, she wanted to cry for him, belonging to no one and no place.

"You don't travel because you want to?"

He shook his head from side to side. The music of his voice was always there, but she'd never heard such a low, sad song played without self-pity. And there was none, only a resignation and acceptance.

"I'm as out of place here as in Ireland. It wasn't different in Borstal or university, New York or Los Angeles. In some ways, it's better now that I'm an expatriate. When people glimpse my feeling, it's put down to the melancholy of the Irish, the stranger in a strange land."

Others might glimpse. Neill was letting her see right into his mind, a gift that gave her both the pain of empathy and the honor of his confidence. Joyce rubbed her cheek on the matted hair of his chest, unsure if the dampness there was the perspiration of their joined bodies or the tears of one woman too close to one man's soul.

"A woman out of time?" she prompted hoarsely. It didn't matter what he said about her as long as she made him change the subject. Poetic or critical, nothing Neill could utter had the chilling force of his blunt, pitiless analysis of himself.

"Oh, yes. You, my timeless woman." A note of happiness rang in his story. One of his legs crossed over Joyce and squeezed her in the muscled vise of his thighs. How many miles had his long legs explored searching for meanings and moments to record?

"Timeless...out of time, not bound by the direction of our time," rambled Neill in between yawns. "This time still glorifies the girl, perpetually, incredibly young but never naive or coy, sexual beyond belief, barely maternal. You are a classic woman, Joyce, but a bit afraid to show it. You're strong and stubborn, willful and indomitable, but all female without cuteness or cloying affectation or phony deference to men. If you were picked up by a warp of time and set down in the past or pushed into the future, you would

See over the page for details

Silhouette Desire

ANNOUNCING SILHOUETTE READER SERVICE

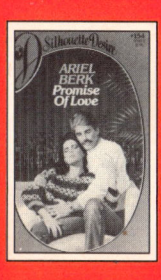

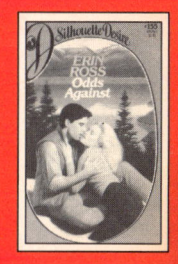

Experience all the excitement, passion and pure joy of love. Send for your **FOUR FREE** Silhouette Desire novels today.

Postage will be paid by Licensee

Do not affix postage stamps if posted in Gt. Britain, Channel Islands or N. Ireland.

BUSINESS REPLY SERVICE
Licence No. CN 81

Silhouette Reader Service,
PO Box 236, Thornton Road,
CROYDON, Surrey CR9 9EL.

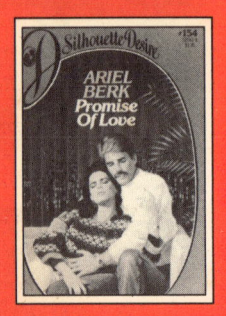

Silhouette Desire are love stories that go *beyond* other romances — taking you behind closed doors, to share the intense, intimate moments between a man and a woman united by love.

These are fascinating stories of successful modern women, who are in charge of their lives and career — and in charge of their hearts. Confident women who face the challenge of today's world and its obstacles to attain their dreams and their desires.

At last an opportunity for you to become a regular reader of Silhouette Desire. You can enjoy 6 superb new titles every month from Silhouette Reader Service with a whole range of special benefits: a free monthly Newsletter packed with recipes, competitions, exclusive book offers and a monthly guide to the stars, plus extra bargain offers and big cash savings.

As a special introduction we will send you Four specially selected Silhouette Desire Romances when you complete and return this card.

At the same time, because we believe that you will be so thrilled with these novels we will reserve a subscription to Silhouette Reader Service for you. Every month you will receive 6 of the very latest novels by leading Romantic Fiction authors, delivered direct to your door. And they cost the same as they would in the shops — postage and packing is always completely Free. There is no obligation or commitment — you can cancel your subscription at any time.

It's so easy. Send no money now — you don't even need a stamp. Just fill in and detach this card and send it off today.

FREE BOOKS CERTIFICATE

NO STAMP NEEDED

**To: Silhouette Reader Service, FREEPOST,
PO Box 236, Thornton Road, Croydon, Surrey CR9 9EL**

Please send me, Free and without obligation, four specially selected Silhouette Desire Romances and reserve a Reader Service Subscription for me. If I decide to subscribe, I shall, from the beginning of the month following my free parcel of books, receive six books each month for £5.94, post and packing free. If I decide not to subscribe I shall write to you within 10 days. The free books are mine to keep in any case. I understand that I may cancel my subscription at any time simply by writing to you. I am over 18 years of age. *Please write in BLOCK CAPITALS.*

Name_____ Signature_____

Address_____

_____ Postcode_____

SEND NO MONEY — TAKE NO RISKS
Remember postcodes speed delivery. Offer applies in U.K. only and is not valid to present subscribers, overseas send for details. Silhouette reserve the right to exercise discretion in granting membership. If price changes are necessary you will be notified. Offer expires 30th June 1986.

2S6SD

thrive, darling. You would be no different than you are now in any time. You would call yourself an ordinary woman whether you were a peasant or a princess, and only a poet would know how special you are."

She laughed, a rippling sound, and kissed his neck and under his jaw, biting his chin. "Very pretty, very romantic, but not historically accurate or psychologically sound. I'd die of drudgery or my own cooking if I were a peasant. I'd die of boredom being a princess."

"I'm a reality therapist, not a mind reader or a dream analyst. My study wouldn't begin to explain you. Someday, there will be books on Riordan and students thumbing through them to write their papers. I'll be lucky if I got a quote."

"Yours would be the only unabridged, authoritative one," Neill said.

Joyce closed her eyes. "I don't kiss and tell." She fell asleep almost immediately with the blanketing warmth of his body and his low laughter all around her.

Seven

The shrill birdlike trill of her alarm woke Joyce, as usual. She reached out and nothing but the cool expanse of linen met her hand. The groggy, heavy feeling was slow to lift, but she knew she had not dreamed the flight back and the night and Neill. No nocturnal imaginings of hers left such vivid memories of color and shape and sound; no erotic fantasy stayed on with a delicious aching in her muscles.

She sat up slowly, peering around, and listened. There was noise, muffled and low, from the kitchen, followed by a few garbled syllables. Neill's shirt was draped limply over the cheval mirror. Joyce slipped into the tatty folds of her green chenille bathrobe and padded as quietly as possible into the living room.

He was pacing the length of her kitchen, clad only in his trousers. The stove light was on; she assumed he had been there for a while, perhaps most of the night. She watched Neill make a circuit of the floor, his eyes fixed straight ahead but unseeing, his hands held together behind his back. His bare feet made a faint whisper as he scuffed them, and from time to time his lips moved, but the sounds, if they emerged, made no sense.

There were critics who said Neill was touched with madness, but it was hogwash as far as she was concerned. By standing quietly, unnoticed, she settled the question of his sanity once and for all within herself. He was writing. On the third or fourth tour, Neill unclasped his hands, scratched idly at the hair on his chest and smiled to himself. He stopped abruptly and bent over something on the counter, his back blocking her view.

Joyce walked up behind him, folding her arms around his waist and pressing her cheek against the warm, broad back. "Good morning, early bird. Or is it night owl? Did you sleep at all?"

"Enough," Neill said in a vacant, distracted tone. His left hand fell to hers and caressed the knuckles, stroked the tapered length of each finger. His right hand worked across a brown paper torn from a grocery bag.

"My eyebrow pencil?" Joyce grimaced and wondered about the strange characters he was printing. "Why do you write in code?"

Neill laughed and threw the eyebrow pencil down. "It's not code, woman. It's Irish, Erse, the Gaelic. I don't want to be read before I'm ready." He pivoted in her grasp, sprinkling her upturned face with kisses and kneading the worn softness of her robe and her shoulders with the air of a contented cat.

Joyce let the kiss deepen and his hands play up and down her back until Neill tugged her very close, fitting them together. In a few more minutes he would be inspired and ready for another creative activity, and she was expected at the clinic.

"Breakfast?" she offered, wriggling out of his hold.

Neill glowered at her briefly, folding up his paper and sticking it into his pocket. "I had something less nutritious but more interesting in mind," he said.

"I have six itsy-bitsies lined up for today. Time and tide wait for no man." She shook the bran flakes box at him and Neill called it cattle fodder, rummaging through her refrigerator.

"A slice of cold meatloaf, milk, and chocolate cake?" She averted her eyes and concentrated on pouring milk on her cereal, suggesting the Wiggins cream cheese and bacon delicacy for unorthodox eaters.

"I'll make us some tonight. Do you want me to come by and help you pack?" Neill asked.

"Am I going somewhere?" Her spoon wavered and then made it to her mouth. "I just got back."

"Moving in," muttered Neil around the hideous mouthful he was chewing. "I can't work here, not really. All my books and papers are at that rented mausoleum and if I brought them here, there wouldn't be room for us to turn around."

"Who said I was moving in?" She choked down a potentially lethal bran flake. "Talk about a fast worker! Neill, we didn't discuss anything about living together. I live here, you live there. Lovers, yes, but roommates...uh-uh."

Neill looked baffled and wet his thumb, chasing down the crumbs of frosting on his plate. "How else will we manage? I have the classes, the tutorials at the house, the folks who come and go, and the book to do. There's no problem with you driving south to north every day to clinic instead of north to south, is there?"

Here we go, thought Joyce, and her stomach jumped. He thought the issue was commuting or not having a car and the only options were your-place-or-mine. Her apartment was her own, her home, her proud and hard-won independence made visible.

"No, that's not the problem," she said, "but we may have bumped into one of those 'little' problems I mentioned last night. Your whole life-style and mine, Neill, well, *incompatible* sort of sums it up."

He argued with her while she was getting dressed but not nearly as ferociously as she expected. Sure, his hours were irregular, his habits like walking all night or leaving his doors open for anyone who wandered in might be different. Joyce didn't have to eat sardines in mustard sauce or put her dresses between the mattress and box spring when she wanted the wrinkles out; she just had to move in.

"I'm not asking you to change," Neill finished. "I'm asking you to be there. All the time I'm free, I want you with me. Is that so unreasonable?"

"It's lovely and romantic and unreasonable," said Joyce. She picked up a rolled pair of panty hose, a white blouse, her crumpled skirt from the floor and chose her words with care. "I'm not ready to make another big decision like this, and living with someone is a big decision. Maybe not to Julia, or to you, or other people, but it is to me."

"We stand on the edge of the twentieth century with half the word leaping from bed to bed and you won't move in with a man who adores you." Neill came down the hall, gesturing dramatically, and knocked a print off the wall. He stepped over it and planted himself in the bedroom door, barechested and barefooted, his hands on his hips. "When would you be ready for such momentous decisions, love? Next month? Next year? Ever?"

"You won't be here next year," Joyce said gently. "When it's right, I'll be ready. Please, trust me! This would be wrong. We'd be at each other's throats in minutes, not months."

She was convinced no woman had refused his offer of bed and board before, because Neill stared at her, incredulous, and his verbal talents appeared to desert him for once. He left her making the bed and swore loudly and inventively from the next room.

Joyce rescued the fallen print and rehung it on her way out. Neill was visibly more self-controlled, and a final lingering kiss before she left almost changed her mind about the virtues of punctuality.

"When will I see you? Tonight?"

Neill shook his head no. The glint of determination crept back into his eyes. "You could see me every night if you weren't so bloody..." He censored himself for a change, and let her go. "No, I have some friends of Michael Boyle's bunking in. They were evicted or some such nonsense and they need a place to stay. And a man who wants me in his anthology is dropping by. To say nothing of my own work, of which, owing to a lack of inspiration, I did not write a line...until late last night."

"Be inspired," she wished him, and added the practical reminder to lock her door when he went to his classes.

"You're a cool one in the light of day," growled Neill. "Somehow I've become the romantic, begging to see you, and you're unmoved, emotionally and physically. Live with me!"

"Not unmoved—practical," Joyce corrected. "I know I want to be with you, as soon as I can and whenever I can."

"So?" Neill yelled at her as she dashed for the elevator.

"You can't always get what you want, to quote the Rolling Stones," she replied.

Their discussion nagged at her all day. Wanting Neill was not the same thing as needing him. It was sheer lunacy to need him, an addiction she could not afford. She lived alone by choice, wary of the kind of relationships where need drove out reason, and dependency was the bond. Julia and Frank couldn't walk around the block without each other, and yet they argued over which direction to go in every time they took a step.

What good could come out of needing Neill or depending on him? He would love her and leave her; she didn't dare to think about the end of the year, but it was real and it was there. She had craved the sight of his face and the sound of his voice on a miserable weekend away. If he was so powerful and compelling a personality, so strong an emotional drug in her system already, how much harder would it be to live with him? How long would she crave him when he was gone?

By the end of the day Joyce's mental gymnastics with her mini-Einsteins and wrangling with her own feelings left her weak. Neill Riordan had become a headache pounding in her temples and she gave in, climbing into bed early and re-reading the bad press Neill had gotten at the St. Patrick's ball. The photo made her laugh in spite of herself.

The pounding was not a dream, not her headache. It went on and on after Joyce sat up, bleary-eyed, and shambled to the front door. Muffled but insistent, Neill's voice chanting her name filled in the gaps between the smacks of his hand on the doorframe.

"Stop that," she said sleepily, undoing the chain with jerky, uncoordinated motions. "Neill, someone will call the cops, if they haven't already."

"Ten thousand pardons," he bellowed down the hall and stepped in. Before she had a chance to object, he enveloped her in a hug that forced the air out of her throat in a gasp. His unshaven cheek pressed hers with a tickling, itchy abrasion.

"It's three-twenty in the morning," Joyce wheezed. "You said you were busy tonight, not to expect you..." She saved her indignation for after his kiss.

He kissed her a little too long and too insistently for indignation to hang around. His tongue moved in to slide with wicked persistence along hers while he took her clutching fingers from the front of her bathrobe to slip his own hands inside. His fingers ran up and down the nightgown's thin material until Joyce could feel the crackle of static electricity and more.

"It is late, isn't it?" he whispered, burying his face in her disheveled hair. "I didn't mean to wake you up...." His hands were bunching up the sides of the nightgown even as he pressed his hips forward to hold her between his body and the foyer wall. "I couldn't sleep."

Joyce was wide awake by now. Neill was moving against her in a way that was not conducive to sleep. "For some reason, I don't think you dropped by for a lullaby"—he slipped one of the shoulder straps down—"or a chat." One of his hands stroked up and down her bared thigh. "Or a cup of coffee."

He nibbled lightly on her shoulder and made a throaty, agreeable sound. The bathrobe was tugged off her while Neill's mouth skimmed down her chest, found one hardened nipple and licked it lazily through the silk fabric.

"It's so late," Joyce whispered. She knew she wasn't going to ask him to leave. Her heart was pounding as loudly and rapidly as he had pounded on the door.

"Wrong of me, I know," Neill murmured, his lips still busy at the tight, aching peak. The humming vibrations went through Joyce like splinters of lightning. "Foolish, too."

His hands slipped behind her to pull her tighter to him. He moved slowly, languidly, letting the taut arousal of his body speak for itself. Neill was not offering an apology or explanation, but himself. His hips tilted and pressed, stoked fire into her stomach, and the heat spread downward while her bare feet felt frozen to the cool tiles.

"Yes, foolish," she agreed in little breathy syllables. "Work tomorrow.... Neill, oh, Neill."

His fingers had turned eager and hungry. It made no sense to pretend anger or reservations when Neill's touches found proof of her own readiness and need. His head rose, his wide eyes were dark with desire and his heart thundered through his shirt as rapidly as hers.

There was no more order or sense to her emotions when he was with her. The knowing persistence of his fingers stroked away every thought but him. Whatever the time, wherever they were, she wanted Neill and he knew it.

"Yes," Joyce moaned softly into the warm, sweet cavern of his mouth. "Yes...hurry."

The trail of his clothes littered the floor all the way to her bedroom.

Last night there had been his restraint. Tonight Joyce wanted none. She wanted to know what Neill was like without control, without a shadowy fear of moving too hard, too fast. He could never teach her boldness if she wasn't willing to learn. And she was much more than willing. She was eager.

His hands were swifter, impatient at stripping away the nightgown, but when the pliant warmth of flesh touched his fingers, Neill was gentle. He drew a lazy, winding path down the length of her from her forehead all the way to her toes.

"I don't want to miss a spot," he said, scooping her up and depositing her on the bed. The little lamp flicked on and he smiled a teasing, taunting smile. "We know where it will end. Show me where to begin."

Slowly, Joyce took his hand and drew it to her. "Here," she said, curving his fingers to cup her breast. Neill's eyes darkened and the tip of his tongue slid across his lower lip as he began to bend toward an erect, pink tip.

"No, here," Joyce whispered, suddenly pushing his hand away and smoothing it down along her ribs. Neill shifted, brought his mouth closer. She waited until the heat of his breath tickled and she could feel the throbbing pressure of his manhood scorching her leg. "Or here," she murmured, pressing his fingers into the satiny skin on her stomach.

Neill groaned, a sound of urgency, and branded her with kisses. His mouth clung and then moved hurriedly while his nails scratched a swirling pattern on the creamy skin. Her hands directed him, led him on from one sweet caress to another, growing bolder as did the whirlpool of pleasure in her gathered strength. Now she sought him, kneading the taut, straining muscles, gently biting at the corded tendons of his neck, his upper arms.

"Darling, let me...let me," Neill moaned, desire and desperation mingled. He was less gentle, grinding himself on her with a rough passion.

He punished her deliciously for each second of delay, his heart racing and his hips showing with each thrust what he wanted. She felt his searing hardness at the moist entrance and arched, stroking him with more fire, glorying in his need as much as her own.

He probed the recesses of her mouth, his tongue filling her the savage way his body trembled to do. She seized his hands and brought them to the wetness between her thighs, inviting their invasion but denying him the fullness of possession. Her own fingers danced on him, finding places of equal sensitivity, burning away the last traces of control.

"Soon," Joyce promised. "Soon but not yet...soon...soon." Her body took up the cadence of the words, writhing under him. She scored his back lightly with her nails, dug them harder into the cheeks of his buttocks. The taste of him was sweet. His weight on her was more exciting than she thought she could stand. He was like sun-warmed granite, pulsating with life.

Joyce gripped his shoulders, pushing and twisting at them. Neill's eyes met hers, seeing the thought before she could even say the words. He rolled back, pulling her with him, pulling himself slightly upward until he could lean his head back against the scrolling metal of the headboard.

"There." He breathed heavily. "Is this the way? Please yourself and let me see you. Oh, Joyce, you're so beautiful like this." His fingers roamed unceasingly and his face was flushed, thrilled with the lovely, proud display she made above him.

Joyce straddled him, lowered herself with an almost cruel slowness until he was sheathed deeply within. His eyes widened, his hips rose and fell as she discovered a thousand new ways to tantalize and move. The control exhilarated her but there was no possibility of restraint. Wave after wave of ecstasy rolled through her in time with the rocking of her hips and the drumming of her heart, now near bursting.

"Oh, now...now, now," she cried needlessly as the explosive final sweetness took her. Neill already knew, for he gripped her waist as tightly as he dared and soared in her while he held her down to himself. She felt the hot surging of his satisfaction, heard dimly the primitive sounds of his own pleasure and let herself crumple and fall on him, exhausted.

Locked together, they lay there until their breathing had quieted. Neill eased his body from under hers and rested next to her, his hands still reluctant to leave. He ran the back of his hand down the length of her spine and let it rest there.

"If I had the strength," he whispered, "which I don't, I'd like to run up and down this respectable building's hallways and tell your respectable neighbors what a wonderful, wanton, passionate lady you are. I'd like to open the window and shout out to a few passersby that I'm your lover."

"The windows do not open in this building," laughed Joyce. "My neighbors are scrupulously uninterested in anyone else. They don't even say hello, as a rule...."

She stopped herself and her laughter. Neill said whatever he liked whenever he liked. He had his own rules for life and love and everything in between; they just weren't always the same as hers or society's. A disturbing thought stirred.

"Neill," she said softly, propping herself up on one elbow to look at him. He was lying very still, his eyes open and staring at the ceiling. "Neill, you can be as earthy as you like but I'm more down-to-earth. I hope you'll understand what I'm going to say. I really think it would be better if we were...well, discreet about being lovers. I'm sure loving you is right; I'm not as sure it's very ethical—not if I ever want to finish and publish my study someday and be taken seriously." *Someday when we're not together,* she added mentally. *Someday when I'm not afraid.*

He didn't blink or move. Joyce thought he might have fallen asleep, but his eyes were wide open, faintly gleaming in the light from the hall. He was right next to her and yet a million miles away. She had seen this look before and it always made her wonder where he was. Sometimes it annoyed or worried her, made her wonder what more of Neill was hidden. Tonight, sleepy and sated with him, Joyce sensed that no matter how public a figure Neill was, there would always be a private Neill, never telling all his secrets. A year would not be time enough to know this man.

She brushed back the thick curls of his hair and pressed her lips lightly to his neck, nuzzling him, tasting the tang of salty skin. He didn't say anything, but his fingers threaded themselves through her hair and idly wound the long, pale ends around and around. His arm drew her back until she was held against his side.

"You didn't hear a thing I said, did you?" whispered Joyce. She closed her eyes and burrowed into the warmth and security of his body, too tired and too content to repeat herself.

"I'm a better poet than you even suspect, love," he murmured back unexpectedly. "I hear all the things you don't say."

Joyce couldn't refuse to meet Julia at the Jolly Burger. Her sister's messages on the answering machine made a lunch sound like life or death. There wasn't a single good excuse to avoid seeing her sister, but the prospect made her uneasy. Julia was sure to ask how things were going with Neill, and Joyce knew she was bound to answer honestly. It was likely Julia would be delighted that her favorite professor and her big "straight" sister were romantically involved, but Julia was hardly the most close-mouthed confidante.

Joyce toyed nervously with her spoon and watched the street outside the grimy restaurant window. With luck, Julia was only in need of more advice on the hopeless, hapless state of her own affair with Frank. Without luck, Joyce and Neill could expect half the university to know about them before nightfall. *Tomorrow, the world,* thought Joyce with a wince.

"Do I look wild with happiness?" crowed Julia. Her hair had a new electric permanent frizz to it. Her lips were bright magenta, almost fluorescent. Her arms were filled with three large packages from fancy Michigan Avenue stores.

"Very wild, at least," Joyce said. She watched Julia dump her expensive burden, her coat and purse into the orange vinyl booth. "You have good news for a change. By your buying switch from Discount City to Saks and Field's, I'd guess you won the state lottery."

"Almost as good. No, maybe better. You know what an incurable romantic I am." Julia lowered her head to study the menu and resembled nothing so much as an enormous scouring pad. "Love is the answer. Haven't I said that all along?"

"Then maybe I'd better rephrase the question," Joyce said dryly. A sinking feeling replaced her appetite for food or Julia's news, but she ordered the first item she saw. "Am *I* any part of this happiness?"

"Well, of course you are!" Julia looked offended.

"Oh, God," moaned Joyce. She wished she had Julia's who-cares attitude, but it wasn't part of her. She wasn't a casual person about life or love; she treasured her privacy. "What have you said about this and to whom have you said it?"

"It's all over the grad school. Ten people must have stopped me this morning to ask if it's true. I couldn't be happier."

Joyce pushed her untouched chicken salad to one side and watched Julia tear into her lunch. "What am I going to do? It just happened. I didn't plan it."

Julia's pickle halted in midair. "What in the devil...of course you didn't plan it. You don't have a blessed thing to do until May."

The two of them eyed each other suspiciously.

"I've been busy moving out of Frank's apartment," Julia finally said, breaking the awkward silence. "I've spent the last week running boxes up to Winnetka to store in our garage at home."

"And you're happy?" Julia's satisfied smile was answer enough. Joyce sighed with relief and patted her sister's hand. "Thank goodness. I never could have advised you to take such a step. The decision was yours naturally, but it does make me happy, too. You'll never regret it. Now, about May... Your graduation?"

Julia was off and running without missing a bite of tuna.

"I told Frank we had to do it. His place was too small, too dingy and terminally depressing. We've fought and fought about it, but he always insisted 'cheap' made up for no windows and 'close to campus' was better than working plumbing."

Joyce didn't care what issue had finally split them. She sipped water and washed away the last of her worries. Julia knew nothing. "Mom and Dad must be pleased. Are you staying there only until graduation?"

Julia gave her a quizzical look as if she'd suggested something indecent. "Why on earth would we move in with them? Dad can't stand Frank for more than ten minutes at a clip. I thought we'd stay with you...."

"We? With me?" Joyce choked on the words.

"Frank and I are getting married," barked Julia. Heads turned in their direction, but she was oblivious. "Are you losing your mind? Mom said she wanted to be the one to tell you last weekend, so I assumed she had. We're getting married May nineteenth. Not Mom and I. Frank and I. Frank's busy looking for a new apartment."

"You and Frank," repeated Joyce dully. She set her water glass down before she dropped it. "I can just see this. You'll wear white satin boxing shorts and go fifteen rounds with

Frank over where to honeymoon. No, you can't stay with me. I've got..."She fished around for something plausible to say. There was no way she could contend with Julia, Frank and Neill all together. "I've got sessions with Neill and I can't have company."

"Fifteen rounds, eh?" Julia looked like a lightweight contender when she asked the question. "You should talk! Frank and I may squabble, but we haven't made the paper with any of our battles."

"That's not fair," protested Joyce. "I told you what happened. Neill and I weren't fighting and no one..."

"Oh, no one can reach you," whined Julia. "No one knows where you are or where you're coming from lately. I thought you'd be happy for us. It's such a conservative, upright, Joyce sort of thing—marriage. Normal!" She sniffled and blew her nose loudly, tears smudging her mascara into black semi-circles. "I'm putting my life in order while you're r-r-running around, acting fl-fl-fla..."

"Flaky?" Joyce supplied while Julia nodded perfect agreement and sobbed.

Julia loved a good scene, and she was doing her best to create one for Joyce and the other bemused diners. She was wasting her tears and deep sobs on Joyce if she wanted to wring her big sister's heart. Joyce had seen this scene played too many times by better actors—her own clientele. Tantrums, eye-rolling, tooth-gnashing and torrential crying neither melted Joyce nor discouraged her.

"Okay, I'm the bourgeois one. I'm Ms. Straight Arrow, but I'm not the one marrying Frank Crowley. In the last six months of living together, you must admit the relationship has been a bit—volatile. If you can face a lifetime of it, fine!"

"I thought you'd be pleased," hiccoughed Julia through the wadded napkins. "Mom was pleased."

"I'm twenty-nine," Joyce reminded Julia softly. "Mother would be pleased to the point of lift off if *I* were marrying Jack the Ripper. But I'm not—marrying or pleased. I wish you would think some more before making such a monumental decision. Are you trying to make us all happy or are you happy?"

Julia actually paused and thought the question over for a full ten seconds. "I'm happy. I'm only hurt that you aren't overjoyed and you don't want me to move in until the wedding."

"Well, pretending has never been my strong suit," sighed Joyce. "As for the roommate business, let me think about it awhile. I don't know if I can stand being referee for a solid month of you and Frank arguing."

"There you go again," shrieked Julia, gathering up her packages and shaking them at Joyce. "You and Neill Riordan are about as similar as oil and water, fire and ice, and you've gotten along with him, haven't you? But Frank and I... Oh, no, that's different. We're in love, but you can't stand to see us together."

"I have." Joyce winced.

Julia drew herself up and prepared to stalk off. "Well, Frank and I happen to agree on a few crucial points. We love each other, we need each other, we're getting married." Her voice grew louder and more strident with each phrase. "And we'll make fabulous parents."

"What?" Joyce knocked over the coffee cups, the salt and pepper shakers and almost broke her hip on the corner of the table, attempting to get out and grab Julia. "Say it isn't so. Say you're speaking in the far future tense."

Julia gave her sister a look of incredible smugness. "In deference to an impossibly bourgeois family, we planned this wedding complete with garden party reception, invitations and you as maid of honor. But by Christmas, you'll be an unplanned aunt. If you were ever home and not working, you'd get your phone messages and return your calls and today wouldn't have been such a surprise!"

On that sour note, Julia made an almost military maneuver and left Joyce standing awkwardly in the middle of the Jolly Burger.

The worst part of the lunch with Julia was not the marriage announcement or the news of her impending niece or nephew. Those events were of Julia's doing, and if they proved to be her undoing, Joyce had very little influence or say in the matter. Even her younger sister's snide characterization of Joyce as an overgrown girl scout didn't hurt or stay with her.

Joyce was a lot less concerned with how she looked to Julia than how she was feeling. She wasn't the way she was—"bourgeois and straight" to Julia, "a go-by-the-rules lady" to Neill—because she thought she *should* be; she just was that way, and she accepted herself. She was painfully shy as a child, cautious as a woman.

Julia's perception of Neill and Joyce as fire and ice, as oil and water, had struck a deep and sensitive nerve. The comparison was too close to the critical way Joyce thought of Julia and Frank for her to ignore. She had to examine her sudden sense of dread in the solitude of her office. For someone who boasted of no acquaintance with tragedy, Joyce felt suddenly the cold winds of doom, an omen in her soul of disaster nearing.

Eight

Joyce had never enjoyed laziness so much. She had never known the delights of torpor before. The sunlight was strong, not early-morning pale. It fell across Neill's bed in short dots and long dashes. Joyce watched until the bright designs crept up her arm, dappled her shoulder and danced into her eyes. She rolled over to shut out the glare and buried her face in his pillow. It held the scent of Neill and soap and her mingled together. There was a sudden flood of the remembered excitement of last night. When his voice came booming up from the bottom of the stairs, Joyce stretched and burrowed deeper into the sheets. She liked being in his bed, and waking up there.

"Come on, woman," called Neill impatiently. His footsteps were climbing toward her thumping on the treads, getting louder, closer. "Breakfast's gone soggy." He called her name until she peeked sleepily back over her shoulder.

"That's the fate of cornflakes," muttered Joyce. "What's my excuse?"

"Too much picnic yesterday and rowing on the lagoon. Too much of a good thing last night," Neill teased. "I'm as happy, tired and sore as a bride myself."

Joyce muffled her laughter under the pillow. "You're as shameless and immodest as people say," she accused.

His slap on her behind didn't hurt, but it was unexpected. The sting made her leave the safe cave of linens and turn around to rub her buttock through the sheet and gape at him. "Tomorrow's your own sister's wedding day," clucked Neill, "and you're not entirely acting the maid of honor, are you?"

"What does *that* mean?" Joyce sat up indignantly, clutching the sheet to her bare chest.

"You haven't told her about us," said Neill. "You haven't told a soul, in fact, even those that suspect. Meeting your family will be awkward all around."

"That's my business," said Joyce. "Julie and Frank didn't care who knew they were in love or living together. I care. I hate gossip and well-intentioned advice, clucking tongues and putting my life on parade. It's *my* life, *my* love."

Neill bent over the bed and tipped Joyce's chin up to kiss her lightly. He studied her finely carved features, the softness of her mouth, and traced the line of her cheekbones with the pad of his thumb.

"*Our* love," he whispered, and his eyes tried to look very deeply into hers. "Do I go to this wedding as your very good friend or your psychological project or your lover?"

"You'll go as you are—as Neill Riordan," Joyce answered. "And if my parents ask, I'll..."

Even as she spoke, Joyce realized she was teetering on the edge of a sheer drop. She was ready to proclaim to the world the words she had hardly dared to admit to herself or to Neill for so long. The commitment was made—they had sealed it with their mouths and hands and bodies. Now she was afraid that when the time would come for Neill to leave, when there would be that ienvitable void in her heart, it would even hurt more if other people knew. She would not be his love, his swan, his darling; she would be only one of his many conquests. There would be the unbearable sympathy and the annoying shaking of heads over poor Joyce, who had finally tripped and plunged headlong into the tragedy of love.

"If people ask," she repeated slowly, "I'll tell them simply that I love you."

Neill smiled and covered her face with light kisses. "You don't have to tell them a thing. They can see it if they're looking. I wanted to hear you say it to me. Sometimes I think you're ashamed of yourself for loving such a disreputable character." He paused. "Or ashamed of me, the unreconstructed rebel?"

Joyce reached for him, her arms raised to draw him to her. The sheet fell down and Neill's hands were on her almost instantly, caressing and sliding over her breasts while her fingers began to work at the buttons on his shirt.

Her hands rubbed across the planes of his chest and she scratched her nails at the round brown circles hidden under whorls of hair until she raised them to tiny hard points. Neill bit a long, light line down the front of her, returning the compliment. The sensations made her squirm and reach for his belt buckle.

"Did you want breakfast or what?" growled Neill, his mouth busy at his own feasting.

"Or what," sighed Joyce. "I'd much rather have 'or what' and you."

Neill was busily scribbling comments on student papers at the breakfast table. Joyce might as well be eating alone. She noticed how deep his concentration became almost immediately. Everything else seemed to disappear for him but the task at hand. It was no different when he was writing his own work or thinking out a problem, but it took getting used to.

"Mush," said Joyce, pushing the cereal bowl across the table.

"Absolute pap," seconded Neill, scrawling that comment on the top of the page in front of him. He fumbled around blindly for his spoon and ate from his bowl and Joyce's in alternate bites.

It was no good trying to talk to him when he wasn't there. Joyce rummaged through his stacks of essays and flipped through a few. Most of them were boring but, sandwiched in the pile, she found a few stapled sheets of a crudely printed newsletter.

The hand-lettered banner proclaimed the paper, *Catha*, and was filled with violent prose and poetry. All of it related to Ireland's civil war and all of it was grim and fanatic. Joyce read it carefully, impressed by the power and passions expressed but horrified by the maniacal, vengeful spirit of the writers.

"*Catha?*" she said loudly. She said it enough times to dent the wall of silence around Neill.

"Gaelic for *tales* of death," he translated, not looking up, turning pages rapidly.

Joyce examined the sheets again, but there was not a single name or organization credited anywhere.

"What is this?" she asked, waving the paper at him, and after her usual difficulty, Neill glanced up.

"Something new on campus. The students pass them around."

Joyce tried to pursue the issue. "Who wrote it? Does it have to do with you being in residence? Is it being distributed in other Chicago colleges?" She grew louder in sheer frustration. Whatever Neill knew or did not know was locked in his leonine head, inside the maze of his mind.

"This is frightening stuff," she insisted, sliding the paper almost under Neill's nose. "Who's behind it? The I.R.A.? Ireland United? Just politically minded students?"

"Leave it alone," Neill said sternly. "If reading it bothers you, put it down. There's plenty of people who hold those views and worse."

She saw something in his eyes she didn't want to see—knowledge. Neill knew more than he was telling. "You don't trust me, do you?" she asked, and of all her questions, it was the most important.

"I'd trust you with my life," Neill said. "I can't tell you what you want to know, and you'll have to trust me in return." His stare was steady and direct, but he was evading her.

"All right," Joyce said slowly, laying the dogeared sheets aside. Love was an act of faith. Sometimes she wondered when her newfound courage would fail her, when she would stop believing it or Neill. "I do."

It was a picture-book day for a wedding. It was a fairy-tale setting in suburbia and Joyce was more nervous than the bride.

The young maple trees in the neighbor's yard shook their tiny leaves like a pastel green fringe of lace. There were no trees in the Laniers' yard; leaves fell and messed up the manicured expanse of her father's lawn, spoiling the immaculate, pruned landscape. There were plenty of late tulips because those flowers had the good taste to bloom without dropping in heaps of dying brown petals. Roses were unruly, sprawling and unwelcome.

It was no accident that Joyce emerged from the comfortable suburban confines of this house and this family without the spirit of adventure. Where nothing was ever broken, no one had to fix anything. Where there was plenty, she never had felt hungry. It was a beautiful cocoon to grow up in but, looking around today, she knew she wasn't ever going to have—or want—such gilded confinement again. She just wasn't as sure of what she did want.

What would Neill make of this niche of respectability? The Laniers' elaborate bows to convention and shows of material wealth disturbed Joyce's sense of justice. She wondered if Neill would make caustic quips after the wedding about a class of people who couldn't look farther than the end of their own driveways, whose dreams were as neat and tidy as their lives, and whose ambitions were measured in annual income.

"Your father is keeping the peace," Mrs. Lanier said as she escorted Joyce into the backyard. "There's no use seating people on the bride's or groom's side when there's a them-and-us division."

Joyce's lips twitched in amusement. The lawn chairs were filling in with guests, and it was easy to see what her mother meant. Julia and Frank had invited their university buddies, the people milling around in blue jeans and bermuda shorts; the family friends, relatives and business associates were a solid block of blue suits and pastel dresses.

"Don't you laugh," cautioned Mrs. Lanier. She smoothed down the folds of her voile and inspected Joyce critically. "You look nice. I should be grateful your sister chose something acceptable for you to wear, I suppose. I had visions, of course, of lace and tulle, linen and pearls but this will have to do."

Neill was nowhere in sight. He had promised Joyce and the blushing bride he wouldn't miss the wedding, but there were times—and this was one—that she didn't entirely trust his word or his memory. Neill was prone to forget, to wander off and end up talking to a stranger or getting lost. She described him to her mother, putting her on the alert to watch for him.

Joyce's mother patted a stiffly sculpted coiffure, where no strand of hair would dare to escape, and peered around the garden. "Your friend," she said with careful, subtle emphasis. "After everything Julia has told us, we're dying to meet this man. Imagine, you and a famous person being...friends."

"Famous is a bit strong. Friends is a bit weak," Joyce said slowly. She had always wanted approval of all the nice men she dated, and it was always forthcoming. It would be pleasant if the Laniers liked Neill, but it wasn't likely or necessary. "Before you ask, the answer is no. He's not the marrying kind."

"All men are the marrying kind," pronounced Mrs. Lanier.

Joyce laughed heartily. "I meant, *I* wouldn't think of it. I took leave of my senses and fell in love, but it's only a temporary lapse. He's here today and gone tomorrow."

"You are courting disaster and your sister is marrying it," snapped Mrs. Lanier. She checked the cloudless blue sky as if it, too, were going to rain on her plans for sheer spite. "What do people have against tradition and doing things the right way nowadays?"

Joyce might have pointed out that Julia was, indeed, walking the very traditional route by marrying a man who dominated her and by immediately starting a family. The sequence was a mite off but the results were the same. She kept quiet and avoided the question. What she felt for Neill was the right thing, but he was the wrong man to love.

"I'll go see what's holding up the show now," Mrs. Lanier sighed. "I'll die if they have changed their minds once more. My nearly new son-in-law won't wear a suit jacket. Your sister won't say the vows the way they're written, as if there were more loopholes in them than in the tax laws."

She bustled off to take charge and Joyce wove her way through the wedding guests to kiss her father.

The last minute complications were, evidently, solvable. Joyce took her place under the striped awning with the wedding party and spotted Neill. He stood far back, at the perimeter of the chairs, refusing someone's offer of a seat with a curt shake of his head. She watched him through the ceremony.

He'd come without a coat or tie. In a tan shirt and brown pants, Neill looked like a tree planted in a desert. He didn't belong to either of the factions here, but when she saw his lazy grin and a conspiratorial wink, an unbidden thought arose. He belonged to her and she belonged to him in a way that defied convention or ceremony.

"For better or worse..."

Mrs. Lanier snuffled loudly into her handkerchief. Joyce felt her own eyes fill. Loving Neill was no temporary lapse, as she blithely suggested. He wasn't going to be torn from her heart as easily as the pages of the calendar.

"For richer or poorer, in sickness or in health..."

The sun glinted off Neill's hair and gave him a red-gold halo. He'll always be on the outside, looking in, Joyce told herself. He'll grow old alone—defiantly alone.

"Till death do you part..."

There was the usual flurry of kissing and hugging, the rising babble of everyone headed in for the reception. Neill waited for Joyce as the guests rushed by him.

"I have seen bigger smiles at a wake and this is a wedding," Neill chided. His lips met Joyce's briefly and he twisted one of the rosebuds from her bouquet, tucking it into his breast pocket.

"I'm too pragmatic for my own good. Marriage is a risky business, at best, and it wouldn't have hurt Julia and Frank to wait. Six months may not be a whirlwind courtship, but it wasn't smooth sailing, either."

"If they had waited much longer, your sister would have to let the seams of that dress out. Smile and lead me to the food, love. My stomach is growling, 'I do.'"

When Neill was in his expansive mood, there was no repressing him. When he was secretive or withdrawn, there was no worming more than a few syllables out of him. A wedding, however, appeared to be one of those occasions where there was no holding him back. Joyce hung behind him a little while his students mobbed him. Their faces always looked to Joyce as though they were slightly tilted when Neill was around them, canted upward to catch every ray Apollo cast on them.

They hung on his offhanded comments as if Neill were something other than a man. A prophet, an oracle, perhaps, Joyce speculated silently. They crowded him, shaking hands and affecting a curious combination of casual but studied disrespect in their banter with him. Under it all, there was an elaborate, hidden deference.

Even Frank and Julia acted awkwardly around Neill. Julia gushed more than usual, if that was possible. Frank did an incredible swagger and show of male camaraderie, while picking apart every last detail of his own wedding.

"How do you stand it?" asked Joyce. "You're not an immortal. You put your pants on one leg at a time, like everyone else." She took his elbow and steered him toward her aunts in hats and gloves and steeled herself.

"I hate it," Neill said candidly. "They want a hero and I'm handy. I'm also handling it a bit better."

"You are?" Joyce sounded skeptical. She wanted to sail past the blue-haired, steely-eyed women, but she didn't dare. She dutifully introduced Neill to each and every one.

Neill made it through the handshaking and initial testing like a champion. It would have been letter-perfect if one of her mother's sisters hadn't asked him what line he was in.

"Marlowe's mighty line," replied Neill, straight-faced. "I used to do dactyls, madam, but the market ran out. I've switched to anapests and they're on the move."

"He's an exterminator," one of the stupefied women said to another. "Bugs, rodents. Think of it!"

They gave Joyce a pitying look. She knew the floor would not open up and swallow her before she died of shame or an explosive lot of giggles.

"Do try Emma's buffet," urged the more tactful of the two. "The Laniers are second to no one when it comes to serving a nice spread. Fourteen kinds of hors d'oeuvres, and from the most fabulous caterer. How does the shrimp sound to you, Mr. Riordan?"

"I don't know," Neill said brightly and politely. He cocked his head to one side and put his hand up to his ear. "They must have very tiny vocal chords. I haven't heard them utter a peep."

Adrenaline gave her strength and Joyce dragged him away.

"You're as red as a shrimp," said Neill. "Does this mean the aunties will never speak to you again as long as you live?"

"No," she gasped, drinking half a glass of champagne in one swallow. "It means they will talk about me for the next hundred years. If you aren't a god, must you be the devil?"

"I'm neither. I'm a man and I..."

She caught his wicked leer, but her parents were bearing down on them too fast to insist on an answer.

Neill was a chameleon, a master at change. Before the color in her throat and face had faded, he managed to dazzle her mother with a judicious application of the blarney and the brogue. Mrs. Lanier hovered like a voile print butterfly targeted on a flower.

Her father gave the appearance of resistance but Joyce knew they were of one mind. There was no dissension, ever, in this household; it was considered messy—like falling leaves—and forbidden. Their marriage was an evergreen where doubts were pruned off.

"My parents liked you," Joyce said as she and Neill left. "You have the gift of making people like you, almost at will."

"It's a survival technique. I used to have to cadge a meal or find a warm, dry hole to curl up in. Being a runaway and a poet, I thought of myself as some kind of bird. I'd flutter around a spot until I was noticed and sing my own song. If they gave me crumbs, I stayed."

Until the crumbs were gone or until the song he sang got him into trouble. She asked him what crumbs he was after today.

"I wanted them to like me because you love them. And loving you is teaching me patience—with the goggle-eyed students, the ones who tell me I must be a fraud or a homosexual or a Communist to be a poet...."

"I'm not going to stay in today," Joyce announced to her secretary as she breezed into the clinic.

"Good thinking," complimented Margaret. "Dr. Kyler's on the warpath about something or other and you've got only Russell scheduled. They ought to make the first day of summer an official holiday, anyway."

"And Pinocchio's birthday and alternate Thursdays for bargain hunting, too," kidded Joyce. She hadn't taken a day off in two years, even during the summer when her work was much lighter with several patients taking off on vacations or being sent to camps.

"What's with you?" asked Margaret. She handed Russell's neatly typed case notes to Joyce and gave her a cautious once-over. She gave Joyce's unusual workday attire of jeans and a peacock blue blouse a nod of approval. "Are you taking Russell on a picnic?"

"Sort of," said Joyce. "Keep your eye out for a Mr. Riordan. Come and get me in the play therapy room. I have to borrow some Monopoly money to take with us."

She was feeling positively jaunty, stuffing her purse with brilliantly colored five-hundred- and thousand-dollar bills. The prospect of spending the whole day with Neill made a nice day nicer and he, at least, hadn't laughed at her newest idea on treating Russell. Dr. Kyler and the boy's parents thought she was a little bit off the wall, but, at this stage, the general consensus was she could try almost anything to reach her patient.

Maybe Neill's influence on her was putting strange notions in her head, but a day at the horseraces had struck her only as unorthodox, not outrageous. Russell was spending more and more time absorbed in his world of numbers, interacting less and less with people. His burning ambition was to become a computer or a calculator and, to that end, he'd begun to talk less frequently and make lots of mechanical noises.

She'd convinced herself there was a kernel of method in her madness. There couldn't be two minds more different than Neill's and Russell's, but she was going on an intuition and a gut feeling. Neill liked children, and given the opportunity, he could talk eloquently and enough for two people. Russell needed something to stir him up; a combination of people and fresh air and racing form statistics and horses might make him more boy and less machine. Neill, as she suspected, was delighted to play hooky for a chance to see the ponies run.

"I found this fellow clanking outside in the hall and measuring your walls," said Neill from the doorway. "I take it, this is Russell."

Joyce smiled at both of them. Neill was speaking more quietly than usual and there wasn't a trace of malice in his words. He had a companionable arm draped around the boy. Russell had knit his eyebrows together and beeped his greeting at Joyce.

"I know you two are going to be a great team," Joyce said, and introduced Neill to Russell. She gave Margaret a wave and the thumbs-up sign and raced for the exit before Dr. Kyler caught sight of them.

The drive out to the suburban racetrack was an education for her. Neill talked a mile a minute about the sport of kings, the value of horseflesh and his boyhood fascination with Irish racing. Russell asked how the odds were fixed and ran Neill's answers, with appropriate sounds, through his information bank.

Another man, Joyce thought with admiration, would dismiss Russell as a "case," but not Neill. He didn't mind differences; he accepted them and, if possible, relished and enjoyed them. She caught herself daydreaming at the wheel, imagining what kind of father Neill would be. It was a dangerous line of thinking.

Today was the first day of summer and the year was more than half over. She blocked off the honeyed sound of Neill's voice and reminded herself that in months, he would be gone. As wonderful as every day and every night they spent together was, it was pointless to allow her own fantasies to grow. She was twenty-nine and in love and more than capable of supporting herself and a child. It could be Neill's child, if she made certain decisions.

But I wouldn't, thought Joyce, glancing over at Neill. He was gesturing out the window, explaining how the course was set up and the differences between runners and trotters. *I know myself too well. I love him too much to deprive his child the pleasure of knowing him. And he would delight too much in his own children to deny him the choice or access to them.*

The realization touched her with a chill, even in the blaze of summer sun. It felt like an omen of the winter to come when she would be cold and alone again.

"Look around!" Neill turned Russell in a circle when they reached their grandstand seats. Russell looked anxiously at the sea of faces, bobbing bodies and the waves of activity. "Don't go all tight on me, boy. Here's the test of our skills, your science and my art. We're here to work the power of your mathematics and my uncanny sense for the beasts."

Joyce laughed and even Russell snickered. She took out paper and pencil and gave Russell his wad of play money, explaining that she would book his bets for him. The boy began to pore over the columns of figures in his program with the gravity of a monk at prayer.

Neill disappeared and came back with coffee and a Coke after a detour close to the rail to study the horses in the paddock. "It's Rivets Runner in the first," he whispered to Russell, "or I haven't a hair on my..."

"Neill," cautioned Joyce. "Russell wants to make his own choices, not learn more about your highly descriptive vocabulary."

"It's got to be Alameda," Russell said, looking seriously, almost coldly, up from his calculations. "I'll bet him to win."

The two sentences emerged without an accompaniment of metallic whirs. Joyce wanted to give a little cry of joy, but she dutifully marked Russell's bet down on her paper and contained herself.

"All right," grumbled Neill. He fumbled in his pocket and pulled out two ten-dollar bills. "Here it is, coin of the realm. You and I'll bet the first five races head to head and then we'll see who has the best system. It's not all in those records and numbers and figures. It's an Irish gift, horse sense."

"Horsefeathers," exclaimed Joyce, trying to reach over Russell to pull the money away from Neill. "A twelve-year-old can't bet! It's against the law. Gambling with a child, Neill!"

"It's all *my* money," he pointed out while Russell gaped curiously at both of them. "The boy's in no danger of losing his inheritance. This is a rather important scientific experiment and a private arrangement between gentlemen. If you were a betting woman, Joyce, you'd go down there and ask all the drivers a few trenchant questions on their psychological state to determine the winner. You ought to do that. Go see if that big bay with the rolling eye has the positive attitude or merely a cast to his eye?"

She couldn't help herself. She laughed and imitated Neill's brogue. "I will not. I'm not going to miss the chance to see you make a horse's ass of yourself."

Russell looked as if he were slightly in pain and Joyce knew he was on the verge of a smile. The carefully cultured blankness the boy usually affected was wearing off despite his nervousness at being in a strange, noisy environment. The anxiety over the new situation and over the huge variety of people was lessening as the boy got caught up in the challenge and the novelty of the activity. And he liked Neill, she noted without surprise.

Russell had reached out and tentatively held onto Neill's arm during the running of the first race. He didn't care for the shrieking and cheering from thousands and thousands of throats and he fixed his eyes on the toteboards, with their comforting, familiar numbers. But he didn't honk or beep or sit down until after the horses and sulkies flashed by.

"Alameda came in second," he said sadly, and did buzz as if something were caught in his gears.

"Well, Rivets Runner nearly died at the post, didn't he?" raged Neill to no one in particular. "I'm out of practice, that's all. I haven't seen them run the Galway Plate in ten years. Sometimes, I think I ought to go back now and then and touch base with what I came from."

Joyce felt the hairs on the back of her neck rise. In all their conversations, Neill had never before expressed a homesickness, a hint of his endless wanderings come to an end. It could happen; he could be mellowing or growing aware of his age and his solitary way. Or did she just want to see that change in him as she wanted to see changes from within her clients?

"Do you mean that? Back to Ireland?" she hollered over the tumult of the crowd. "For a visit, you mean. You told me it was either Iowa or Florida for next year's stint."

"Iowa...Iowa," muttered Neill, and he ran his finger down the racing form. "Here it is, Corn Maiden and the silks are yellow. No, not for me. I'm strictly potatoes." He leaned over and kissed Joyce right in front of a stupefied Russell. "I'd like to spend Christmas with my brother, Eamon, this year. You ought to take a vacation and go with me, Joyce. You'd find him fascinating; he's practically certifiable."

She demurred and put away the shiver of false hope. Neill wasn't changing. He was constitutionally incapable of settling down, of organizing and planning his future the way other men did. He drifted happily in the currents of life, while she was anchored solidly to her work here.

Russell finished making a bizarre series of winding motions with his hand and cranked out his decision. "I pick Patsy's Bright Star in this race. I want to double my bet, Dr. Lanier."

"Did you hear that?" crowed Neill. "The boy's a sport." He nudged Russell conspiratorially. "I can read those wins and losses, times and finishes, too, but all the numbers in the world aren't worth a tinker's damn, Russ. It's not the odds, it's the feeling you get."

"And what feeling do you get?" Russell appeared shocked at the criticism of his ideal universe of percentages and integers and logarithms. Joyce was grateful for any human expression that Russell assumed.

"You have to look for magic," counseled Neill, but he was looking at Joyce as he spoke. "Once you feel it, you know you're right or headed that way."

It still surprised her how much Neill could convey with a certain persuasive gleam in his eye or the way his hand found hers and held it. After these many weeks as lovers, she expected there to be a lessening of the thrill, the anticipation, even, perhaps, the desire. It didn't dim or die. She could read his wordless invitation and her body's quick acceptance, an eager burst of heat and light from some internal sun.

"I feel like I should be running in the third," muttered Joyce, but she left her fingers entwined with Neill's to savor the secret flow of warmth between them. It couldn't hurt Russell to see some evidence of human affection, not machine efficiency. "Check and see if Lost Her Marbles is listed. She's slow starting but hangs in there in rough conditions."

Neill laughed when Russell reported solemnly there was no such horse and the track was rated perfect today.

By the end of the fourth race, Neill was slightly ahead of Russell. He promptly sank his own credibility and theory by putting his meager winnings on Killeen in the fifth. The virtues of the horse's name, the green and gold silks, and Neill's hoarse exhortations from the stands failed miserably and lost him his edge. Russell prudently chose the favorite and won. Joyce got a vicarious thrill when Russell managed a real, if puny, cheer that was one hundred percent boy-inspired.

"The miserable and poor-spirited loser will buy ice cream on the way home," said Neill. He made a dramatic gesture and showered everyone around them with the confetti of his pari-mutuel tickets as they left.

The stop at the crowded ice cream parlor was Neill's idea, not hers. Russell settled for a single scoop of vanilla and attracted lots of attention from the other children by walking around, relieving his anxieties by clicking, clanking and humming.

"I'm not so sure about this," warned Joyce. "Russell is almost on overload after the races and he's done remarkably well. I don't want to push him."

Neill glanced over and returned the icy stare of an annoyed man. "Let him be for a while and risk it. He's a nice little robot, isn't he? I'll bet his folks keep him locked in a closet and take him out only to balance their checkbook."

"That's part of it," admitted Joyce. "Ever since they discovered what a mathematical whiz he was, Russell's parents pushed him to the max."

"And he's got no way to turn them or himself off," Neill guessed. "He feels like a machine, so he acts like one."

"Very perceptive," Joyce complimented. "You would have made a terrific psychologist."

"We're not so different, you and I," Neill said. "I explore the magic of the mind and you explore the maze."

She should have protested there and then. They were different and the differences spelled the end of such quiet moments of sharing, such days together, like today. If Neill were not so different, he would not be able to love her only for now, knowing he was leaving. Loving Neill did not feel like a temporary condition; she knew it would not end with the new year. Perhaps the feeling would never end. Watching him with Russell and Lisa had made Joyce want his child, but a child meant commitment. Loving him made her want Neill for all time.

Neill didn't talk much about commitments. Poetry, love, yes. But as he had told her, "There aren't any rules I follow." Joyce thought about all the rules she'd made for herself and followed and how dull the game would seem after Neill.

"You look sad," he noted, caressing her shoulder. "Tired? Discouraged?"

She licked a drop of ice cream off her finger and shook her head in denial. "No, today went very well. I was just thinking about this year. I can't remember one as wild, as unpredictable, as upsetting...or as wonderful." She smiled into the inviting vista of his eyes and let herself enjoy the sight of him. The only rule for her now was to take each minute with Neill and live it fully. "Today's the summer solstice. The year's half over."

"You're a pessimist," scolded Neill. "The year's just begun." He got up and put Russell on hold gently before he went to pay the check.

Joyce dropped the boy off and got no response to her offer of dinner. Neill had fallen into one of his silent, distracted moods. He said he wanted to take one of his long walks and he would show up at her apartment later.

"Do you want company tonight?" offered Joyce. "That way, I can be sure you won't wander by and wake me up at three in the morning."

Neill leaned down and stuck his head through the open window of the car, kissing her. "I don't know when I start out where I'll end up or when, but I have to go alone. Don't bother to fix me any dinner."

"I won't," said Joyce, "but you'd better remember one scientific fact about the first day of summer."

Neill held her face between his hands, studying it as if he, too, were memorizing her for the future. "What's that, love?"

"This is the longest day of the year, the longest day we'll spend together...and the shortest night."

Neill let his lips brush the corner of her mouth. "I'll try and hold that thought," he promised.

But she spent the night alone. There was his call, late and short, with the sound of longing strong enough to make Joyce dream of him. The evenings they did not spend together were almost as precious to her as the ones they shared. Neill was untouchable, unreachable when he was absorbed in something, but there was always his voice, low and intimate, reaching out to her before the night ended. For a man who remembered neither keys nor wallet, it was an impressive show of love.

It was not fair to compare Neill to any other man who had touched her life, but she did. When a day at the clinic drained her of everything and it would take hours of quiet and solitude to recover, she could tell Neill and not see a suspicious look of hurt, not hear the note of rejection. She didn't have to plead for herself as she had, even with Alan, "This has nothing to do with you. I have to be by myself for a while."

What they had together was growing too good. Each space between them—even a night alone—made the next time more wonderful. By now, she knew the next time they were together, no matter where, there would be the spark all over again, the sense of the first time. She had finally met a man as strong and committed to his life as she was to hers. They were as different as day and night but good together.

It doesn't have to make sense, Joyce concluded, because it won't last. They were on a collision course, with time running out. Their strange alliance would, unlike Julia and Frank's, produce nothing but poignant memories.

Nine

"You can fry an egg out there on the sidewalk, if that's how you like them," chuckled the announcer on Joyce's clock radio. "We're well on our way to the longest, hottest summer..."

Joyce clicked the radio off and finished making the bed. Neill had been gone long before the sun was even up, nuzzling her to the dim state between wakefulness and sleep with his good-bye kisses. He'd said things that didn't register, but she found two tickets to Orchestra Hall for tonight on his pillow.

Mornings like this were dreamlike. The hottest summer on record was only appropriate to match what was becoming the hottest affair on record, Julia had hinted broadly the last time they talked.

A navy sundress looked like a safe bet for today. Joyce put it on, noticing the faint discoloration on her thigh for the first time. Neill, my demon lover, she thought. It didn't hurt and it wouldn't show but she would know it was there, marking her in secret as his.

There were times lately when she wanted to tell everybody. It was probably some delayed adolescent feeling, like collecting a hickey above your collar to show the world that someone loved you. She didn't want Neill to be a secret vice, a discreet interlude in her life. She didn't want him to fade, unnoticed, like a tiny bruise.

Hanging up on Julia was a nasty trick. Joyce made a mental promise to call her tonight and apologize. But it was not the hottest affair on record. For the most part, it was still off the record, a private kind of madness that burned brighter and brighter and made Joyce want to tell people she bumped into on the street how wildly happy she was. While she was at it, she would tell Julia that marriage certainly had had a deleterious effect on her. A scolding, cautious, matronly Julia was not any easier to deal with than her former wild-eyed, bushy-tailed self, and lots less fun.

"Hope your friend has the luck of the Irish. He's going to need it," sighed Margaret from behind her morning paper. She peeked over the edge of the *Tribune* and gave Joyce such a sympathetic look, Joyce snatched the paper, half-expecting to see Neill's name in the obituaries.

Joyce swung away from Margaret's desk, unable to stand her secretary's pitying stare, unable to comprehend the bold words. There were names and Neill's among them. She read the list and there were others she recognized—people Neill had mentioned, people she had met casually, like Michael Boyle. She felt faintly sick at the headline announcing indictments sought, and the figures and the letters blurred without warning.

Margaret's voice, anxious and apologetic, sounded as if she were standing at the far end of a long tunnel. "I'm sorry; I thought for sure you'd know about this. All these people raising money for arms or buying guns for Ireland... It's shocking!"

"Yes," Joyce muttered through bloodless lips. Her fingers turned to stiff, wooden sticks. *I can't believe it,* she started to say but it came out, "I can't see anybody today."

The feeling of panic gripping her made further speech impossible. What did she believe? The tiny black letters became clearer and formed strings of dark pearls, citing reliable sources in the Justice Department and saying Neill and those others listed could be indicted for serious crimes. It was a mistake. It had to be. Another case of "Poet Packs A Punch," she thought wildly, but the panicky feeling would not subside.

"It's okay," Margaret offered weakly. "Go home and I'll make up an excuse for Dr. Kyler and cancel your patients."

"Don't lie," insisted Joyce. "Tell him I was upset about my...friend." *My friend but so much more, too.* Had love blinded her completely to Neill's flaws and imperfections? She was clutching the paper as tightly as she was holding on to every minute of her time with Neill, unwilling to let it go, praying this would be the longest summer on record.

She started toward her office and rejected Margaret's repeated injunction to go home. She couldn't. It would be sheer torture to pace the floor and wait to hear from him. There must be something she could *do*. Her desire for action scared Joyce as much as the article had shocked her.

With the newspaper spread out on her desk and her door locked, Joyce bent over the words and tried to sort out what was happening—not just to Neill, but to her. Outside, the city was sweltering as the temperature was soaring toward a new record. Here, in black and white, she could see the fires of confrontation and trouble facing Neill. Inside her, there was a burning wish not to take refuge in the planning, the careful thoughts, that always marked her before.

"The darker our fortune, the brighter our pure love burned," quoted Joyce. Her ball-point pen scrawled the words in the margin of the paper, and after a minute she recalled it was from Thomas Moore, a poet she had slept on before she'd slept with Neill. It wasn't only the joyful, silly, passionate times she wanted—she wanted forever, the one thing he could not give.

She fought down her impulse to call him immediately. The scoop required her close reading three times, words and phrases leaping out like physical blows. "Conspiracy to export firearms and implements of war" conjured up grim pictures. Newsreels of Northern Ireland ran in her head while Neill's powerful poetry rang in her ears. "Wiretap evidence" made her think about those nights when she hadn't seen him and they had been able only to whisper a few very soft, very private thoughts to each other on the telephone.

Those endearments might be on tapes along with gun deals and fund-raising plans for civil war. The nights Neill spent in her arms, whispering the tender, wonderful words of a lover might have been interspersed with nights spent with these other men. She'd met angry, fanatical men, men he knew, speaking in bitter words, making bloody deals for a war half a world away. Neill was a man of many moods and feelings; she had seen his anger and the bitterness, the restlessness, the loneliness that he showed to very few. Was he also a hypocrite, writing the most moving, dramatic lines for a literary audience and the violent, hate-filled *Catha* paper for another group?

The answers were not found in the newspapers, only the allegations. She wouldn't find answers in the slim volumes of his books. And she didn't want to wait to hear the verdict handed down at a grand jury hearing or in a deportation order from Immigration. She wanted Neill to tell her, face-to-face.

Joyce's fingers were shaking so badly when she dialed his number, she had to ask the operator to put the call through. The mechanical recording informed her that her call could not be completed. "That number is temporarily out of service."

The street in front of his house was clogged with people. She recognized some of the university students. The reporters and cameramen were easy enough to distinguish and the few others might well be police or government officials. Joyce tried to talk to a few of the students, but they were too busy debating Neill's credibility and future to pay much attention.

"They'll cancel his seminars," one said. "It'll ruin the damn semester for us."

For us? Joyce thought she would scream like a banshee at the student. Neill's whole life and career might be in ruins. She pushed her way forward.

"I hope it's true," another student was telling her friend. "I knew all this apolitical garbage was just that! Garbage! He's Irish. A man like him *has* to have causes to fight for."

Joyce wanted to cry. Neill described himself as part of the world and belonging to everyone while not held fast by anyone, any one place. He said he hated his rare interviews because his work spoke for him better and clearer than the trivial details interviewers dwelt on. Was he a liar, too?

"Neill," she called, knowing it was hopeless. He wasn't going to hear her single voice above the chatter of the curiosity seekers. "Neill!"

In desperation, she circled the block and threaded her way through the alley behind the rowhouses. Looking over her shoulder anxiously, jumping at the unexpected bark of a chained dog, everything she did gave her the feeling that she was caught in some very bad spy movie, but she had to see him.

There wasn't anyone lurking behind Neill's house. Joyce tried the kitchen door, and it swung open without resistance. Not everyone knew that Neill no more locked his house than he guarded his tongue. She slipped in and closed the door noiselessly behind her.

The kitchen table was overflowing with his papers and books. The sink was filled with unwashed dishes and cups. Neill wasn't there, bent over his writing. The phone was lying on the floor, thrown against the cabinets hard enough to leave a scar on the painted wood.

"Neill," she whispered, peering into the darkened living room. It took her a minute to see him, standing at the curtained window. He dropped his hand and the tiny slit of light in the drapes closed.

"Bloodsucking leeches," Neill said without turning to face her. He didn't sound surprised to hear her voice. "You shouldn't have come here, love. There's nothing here but trouble."

"There's you," Joyce amended. She couldn't read the expression on his face as he left his post and came to her. If she was expecting to read guilt or innocence easily, she couldn't. "What's this all about?"

Neill stopped short of her, unable or unwilling to take her in his arms. He gave a short laugh, harsh and humorless. "The fulfillment of a family prophecy, I believe. The Riordans always claimed I was born to end in a high place. The gallows qualifies."

She understood the black humor too well. He might as well be hanged if he was guilty. There wouldn't be too many places willing to have him teach; there wouldn't be too many readers or publishers willing to take the poetry of a disgraced, deported poet seriously. He would make great copy for the scandal papers, but his third book—and the ones after—wouldn't be acclaimed.

Joyce went to him, wrapping her arms around his waist and leaning into the tense rigidity of his body. "I had to see you. I tried to call but..." She gestured with her head back to the kitchen. "You pulled the phone out."

"Wiretaps," he said angrily. "People following me and taking notes on where and who and what. I go where I want and I talk to whom I please. I say what I like when I'm moved to speak. You know that."

His face became fierce, grim. The gray eyes Joyce had seen tenderness and passion in a thousand times were cold and bottomless. There was no sparkle, no life to them. He was capable of hatred and anger, but she could not bear to think of him capable of dishonesty.

"You should go now, while you can," he said in a thickened, pained way. "This nonsense will last for months, dragging on, dragging me down. I don't want it to touch you. I don't want it to spoil what we've had together."

He was probably right. She should leave. Just as the wildness of this man had changed her, it was likely his difficult course ahead would affect her if she stayed too close. A taste of Neill, and everything was different. She should run back to the order and security of her own life.

Cautiously, Joyce lifted her lips to his and kissed the thin, tense line of his mouth. "Nothing can spoil what we have when we're together, Neill," she said, meeting his bleak eyes fully.

"Don't talk like a fool. That's my role," pleaded Neill. "I've been in and out of scrapes and trouble for years. The press loves it, but you won't. I'll ride it out. You ought to be safe and warm, not muddied or battered by a storm you've got nothing to do with."

He was absolutely right, Joyce decided. Being with him had been a season of storms, a slew of hurricanes, a new world of constantly shifting emotional weather. She would never be the same after this year.

"I'm not going," Joyce said. The words popped out of their own volition. She hadn't planned or thought about what she said. "You don't really want to get through this mess alone. I'm here. I'm staying here."

"You're crazy," Neill said, but he put his cheek on the top of her head and hugged her. "I fell in love with a sane, sensible woman—a lovely, regal swan swimming placidly—and now she wants to act like a goose. Do you have any idea of what's in store for you? For me?"

"None," Joyce admitted. It didn't seem to matter, either, when they were holding each other. For once, the unknown was preferable to the known. If she didn't stay with Neill through the torment of hearings, indictments and accusations, she would not see much of him. That prospect was more frightening than anything else she could imagine.

He stood there quietly for several minutes and Joyce felt the tension of his body slacken a bit. The sounds of the people outside floated in, a few students chanting his name, the honk of a car trying to get through. He became stone once more.

"It won't work," he said with finality. "You move in and they'll slap you on the front page. They might have you in court, testifying to all the who and what and where of my days...and nights. Think of your parents' reaction and the dear old aunties when they discuss us at Mah-Jongg. Chiefly, you have yourself and your career to think of, Joyce."

She brought her fingers up and let them rest on his cheek. "I have. Who's better qualified to offer support than your psychologist? Who's more motivated to be with you in times of stress and strain? We made a deal, Riordan, for a year's study. My time isn't up yet."

"I think it is," Neill insisted sternly, but she could see the struggle in his face. He grabbed her hand and kissed each long, tapered finger with a lingering tenderness. "So far, it's been minor-league madness between us, bite and scratch, kiss and make up. With my back to the wall, it will get ugly and you'll only get hurt."

When had he become the sensible one? When had he stopped acting on a whim and doing the first thing that came into his head? With a start, Joyce realized she hadn't asked him the most important question. Was he guilty? And she was almost past caring about the answer. This was Neill, and separation from him was uglier to contemplate than whatever the truth was. But she had to ask.

"Have you done anything wrong?" Her eyes searched him, seeing nothing but good in his rough, wonderful features.

Neill's hands held her shoulders, tightened as if he would shake her, but then dropped listlessly to his sides. A shadow of darkness crossed his face.

"Numberless things in my life," he croaked. He looked away from Joyce and back again. "I've told you about most of them, haven't I?"

"But *this*! The gun-running, the money for arms, that *Catha* business..." Her voice quavered and died. She didn't want to say what she did not want to believe.

"I write about the helpless and the powerless," Neill said, his bitterness cutting through the natural sweetness of his brogue. "I don't put rifles in their hands and I sign my name to what I write. There's no more to say about it. You've gotten what you came for and that's more than any of them—" he swung his thumb toward the street "—will get. What's keeping you here?"

It certainly wasn't six feet one inch of glowering Irishman. Neill was making it clear—all too clear—that she was expected to bow out. Trouble was his specialty, not hers. Neill made waves and Joyce had spent years spreading oil on troubled waters. Yet, she was the one ready to jump in, move in.

Call his bluff, she thought suddenly. If it was over, she needed to know. She wanted every second of this crazy year with this extraordinary man, whatever it cost.

"Tell me to go," Joyce said bravely. "I couldn't say those words to you, not once since we've been waltzing around in each other's lives, not when you call me in the middle of the night to give you tea and sympathy, not when you've led us both in and out of some weird scenes and shown up at my door whenever you want. We always manage to end up together. You weren't even surprised when I showed up today. You were expecting me. Okay, tell me to go."

"Don't ask me to say it," Neill said, but there was a plea in his eyes. "You know as well as I do that you should go. Do it and be done with me."

Someone began a steady knock on the front door, calling Neill's name. He motioned slightly with his head in the direction of the racket. A loud voice demanded a statement for the local news.

"It's only beginning," Neill warned her. "I'll say it..."

She eliminated that possibility in exactly the way Neill had cut her off so many times. Her mouth met his hard, matching any kiss for ferocity and hunger that he had ever given her. Her tongue was the aggressor, slipping in to drain away his resistance.

The regular thumping on the door reminded her of how many times Neill stood outside her apartment, demanding she let him in, not make him go. "Riordan, Channel Nine.

Isn't there something you want to say in response to these allegations? Channel Nine!"

"Joyce," moaned Neill, gathering her tightly to himself. His lips began to slide and twist on hers but his hands came up to hold her upper arms, as if he still thought he could push her away when the kiss ended.

He was strong and stubborn but Joyce had never felt such a sense of her own power before. Neill was the one who had tapped the depths of her womanly passion, made her experience the boldest, limitless desires. He would have to contend with her before anyone else.

"Say 'I want you to go,'" she demanded breathlessly, keeping her lips fractionally away from his. Deliberately, she arched into him, letting him feel how little clothing separated them, a layer of shirt, a thin sundress.

"I want..." Neill began softly. His hand ran down the back of the dress and his fingers settled around the round, warm curve of her buttock. Joyce moved forward until the button on his jeans pressed into her.

Neill tried again as Joyce's fingers skimmed down his body and slipped between them to tug at the offending metal rivet. "I want you..."

"So I notice," she said, touching him through the denim, feeling his body grow in strength even as he was weakening.

The melée on the porch intensified. The pounding was so loud, it sounded as if the door would splinter. "WGN mini-cam crew, Mr. Riordan. If you'd step out here, sir..."

"If you would step upstairs, sir," Joyce said quietly. She felt both panic and passion. It would end here, now, unless they loved and trusted each other enough to go on. Twisting one arm behind her, she pulled at the dress's zipper and felt the fabric part and begin to spread. Her fingers rubbed him lovingly, stroking as if to soothe but succeeding only in making his hard contour more prominent.

She saw, not heard, the debate Neill had with himself. His brow was damp and creased. His eyes were still chilly, but his hips shifted to press himself tighter into her palm. His tongue came out to wet dry lips and Joyce wet her own mouth, deliberately, provocatively.

"I want you to..." Neill began in a firm voice. His hand rose slowly and his fingers slipped under the thin strap over her shoulder. "Take off that damned dress," he moaned.

"And nothing could stop me," Joyce said. With one tug she lowered the dress to her waist and something wild, primitive and wonderful filled her, knotted her nipples into two hard, pink buds ready to burst at his touch.

"Upstairs," Neill suggested through clenched teeth.

Even as Neill took her arm and led her, the mini-cam man was yelling, banging his fist on the door.

"Love at noon," she said softly. "Film at ten-thirty."

Last night she had slept alone. Neill had gone to bed with the Newberry library and half his wardrobe. Joyce circled the bed, stepping over debris, and kicked off her sandals. Her dress followed, but when she saw Neill, she stopped, leaving the white lace and nylon triangle of her bikini on.

He had taken off only his shirt. His hands were poised at the waistband of the jeans, but static. There was need but there was reluctance, too.

Joyce went to him, sliding her hands up his arms until they met behind his head. Her fingers searched and found the telltale stiffness in his neck, the unyielding ridges of muscle along his shoulders. Slowly, the small circles she drew on him began to meet less resistance. She took a step forward and brushed his chest with the quivering, aching tips of her breasts.

"We doctors have healing hands," she said, stretching up to let their lips meet. "Put yourself in my hands." She made her tongue dart and swirl in his mouth until his began to duel, to seek her.

"Only your hands?" Neill asked when she tipped her head back. "There's healing here." He took another kiss, deeper, more drugging and sweet. "And here." His fingers grazed the front of the panties and slipped between the softness of her thighs.

"First, hands." She opened his jeans button and slid the zipper down, freeing him of the material's confines. She sank slowly before him as the denims descended, taking his briefs with them and making him step out to stand before her.

Joyce looked at him as Neill always looked at her body: open, direct, making no secret of the delight she took in such virility and beauty. With infinitely light strokes, she touched him, following the line of hair from his chest to his navel, caressing the line of solid hip, the slight hollows of his pelvis, the flat plane of stomach. His whole body shuddered when Joyce outlined the flex of each thigh to his knees and began to rise upward along the inside path to his waiting, pulsing manhood.

"Oh, God," Neill said harshly. "More. Touch more, love. Ahhh, yes. More."

She loved him gently with her lips, her mouth, her hands, while he held her tightly to himself, one hand gripping her like iron at the shoulder, one hand clutching desperately in her hair. Her own body flowed with his excitement, trembled and burned with as much pleasure as she gave.

Neill made a sound, deep and pained, and, twisting away, bending down, he lifted Joyce to her feet. He was man and animal both. Wildly, he pushed her down on the bed and wildly his hands opened her knees, made a place for himself. There was a madness in his face, but it was wonderful to see.

Joyce kissed the vein pulsing in his throat, felt him enter her with a single demanding thrust and responded, moving with her own need. Her legs wound around him, trying to take ever more of him, trying to hold him forever. Joyce cried his name at the convulsive moment of release and felt him carried with her.

She went to some other place, a paradise without a name, not on any map. There was only trust and love to take her there, and she could reach it only with Neill, she felt sure.

"I'm stupid with contentment," Neill said. He licked the nape of Joyce's neck and bit her very gently, the love nip of a lion. "I wanted you here so badly. I wanted to be able to ask you to stay, but I wouldn't have."

"Why not?" She wriggled out of the tangled sheets and swung her legs over the side of the bed.

"This is my problem, not yours. I've always managed on my own before. There wasn't anyone to love or protect, so I could run or stand and fight. It didn't matter."

"And now?" She looked over her shoulder as she pulled on her clothes. Neill was propped up on one elbow, making no secret of his enjoyment, watching her dress. "I'm moving in to be with you, Neill. You don't have to take care of me."

"I know that. I want to take care of you, and asking you to stay is damned hard because of that. You're the strong one in lots of ways. Secure, steady... It's not supposed to be this way, you know. I haven't given you anything but grief with the promise of more to come."

She laughed and peeked out of the upstairs window. There were only a few people wandering aimlessly around in the street below. "Funny, but I don't feel grief-stricken. If I didn't have to drive over and get my things, I'd get back into bed and show you."

"Ah, you lust after me." Neill grinned. "I couldn't believe you downstairs, seductive, bold, a temptress a man dare not refuse. What in the world has come over you?"

"You," she said blithely. "You were supposed to teach me daring and you succeeded."

"Beyond my wildest expectations," Neill added.

"Okay, what do I bring? My cribbage board, my recipe for Irish stew or a cattle prod?" Joyce bent down to grab a scrap of paper from the floor. There were a few things she did not want to forget. She looked around for a pencil.

His horrified roar from the bed proved to her the possibility of one's heart leaping into one's throat. Neill was on his feet and nearly incoherent with fury. She didn't think she had ever seen him as agitated or livid before. She looked around for an intruder, but it was the piece of paper in her hand that Neill was pointing at.

"My work! Never touch it! I don't lock the doors and I won't. A thief can have it all. All but the words."

The paper was written on, but so were half the sheets littering the carpet. Joyce faced Neill down and waited until he was through. His temper was short-lived but spectacular.

"There's no better place to study a lunatic than in his asylum," she said, handing him back his paper. "I think I've just committed myself, voluntarily."

When Neill spoke, his voice was tense and strained. "Only the words are valuable. The words and you. But it's not too late. You can reconsider, love."

There wasn't anything to reconsider. She saw the slightly haggard look on his face and understood another fear he didn't want to own. The real fight was coming, and he thought she should be spared.

"I'm here because I want to be," Joyce said. "I'll stay unless you won't have me." She smiled crookedly, and decided not to make it too easy on him, either. "But, Neill, you're going to have to clean up your act and clean up these damned papers."

Ten

"Who are those people camped outside on your porch?" Joyce inquired casually. She brought in her single suitcase and a hair dryer, having decided to travel light. "Being footloose, you seem to attract gypsies."

She could have added, *And pass the tradition on*, but she didn't. Except for conferences and a random, rare weekend away, Joyce hadn't roamed very much.

"Students. The Riordan defense league," Neill said. "They'll keep potential window-breakers at bay, I suspect, until they get tired and give up."

When Joyce asked what the students wanted, Neill shrugged. "A lecture, an explanation, an impromptu reading. Who knows? My experiences lately have taught me that everyone wants something from me. *Nearly* everyone," he amended himself. "I haven't figured out what the devil you're after but aggravation."

"A chance to test my newfound daring," Joyce suggested. "There's probably a better way, like sky-diving, but this will have to do."

Neill laughed and hugged her tightly. It hurt. Her tension and apprehension was so strong tonight, he could probably feel her brittleness, her ambivalence. Neill unwound her fingers from the suitcase handle and hefted it.

"We started off on the wrong foot, but that's my fault," he said bluntly. "I'm sorry for my shouting this afternoon." He swept his free hand in an arc, urging Joyce to take a look.

There wasn't a book or a piece of paper anywhere in evidence. Neill jerked his thumb toward the kitchen before she could ask what happened, and pronounced it off limits to her. His writing room was sacred and the hell with cooking.

"We'll have to eat, won't we?" Joyce peered around him and covered her eyes in mock horror. The table, the counters, every inch of space was taken up with his work. "Scratch that. There's plenty of restaurants and take-out places."

"The dining room's all yours," offered Neill expansively. He led her from room to room, dragging the suitcase with him, and they negotiated as they went.

It wasn't until much later, surrounded by cartons of Chinese food, that Joyce realized what monumental events today marked. Neill Riordan had been seduced, cleaned house, taken a roommate and...

"You apologized!" She dropped her fork and fished it out of the sweet and sour pork in shock. "You said you were sorry."

"I know what *apology* means," Neill said gruffly. "I'm not entirely without a vocabulary, y'know." He quickly stuffed a piece of egg roll in her mouth and made fun of her table manners. The sticky pink sauce was dripping down her sleeve.

Joyce let it go. Moving in with him promised disaster earlier but his apology, unprecedented and unexpected, threw her for a loss. All bets were off as to what would happen from here on. The simplest, glib phrase that other people used to slide through, to get by, did not come easily to Neill. He'd hurt her and he made amends. He never modified his behavior to suit fashion or fad, but only himself. He was changing and she'd nearly missed it. The loss of distance had weakened her powers of observation and objective analysis, Joyce duly noted in her journal that night.

For that loss, there were compensations. She failed to record for posterity how much she laughed, how great it felt to be serenaded on a silver penny whistle by a naked man. She didn't think the psychological community would much care that Neill bayed and swore and screamed all alone in the kitchen because his work was going badly but that he never again raised his voice in anger to her. But Joyce cared deeply.

And each time they made love, it forged a tiny gold link between them. There were no chains lighter to wear than his arms around her every night. There was no metal stronger or more valuable than his flesh—hard, proud, moving inside her body. There was nothing that could tarnish the moments of purest sharing when their spirits flowed and blended in love's fiery crucible and became one.

She could not let herself forget that however long the chain and short the distance, it would break and Neill would go.

"Things have a habit of going from bad to worse lately." Joyce observed a few days later. She read him the latest account of Riordan's own arraignment. He'd made a memorable speech, quoted almost in full, denying any guilt in the case but admitting proudly that he had friends of every political persuasion in nearly every country he'd lived.

"I got a small round of applause for my remarks," Neill boasted. He moved the curtains slightly aside and peered out into the street. "I don't see anybody waiting or any spying reporters. You'd best get going to the clinic before they arrive."

"And what are you planning to do today?" What could he do? Joyce wondered. His summer seminars had been suspended, pending the outcome of the grand jury and Immigration hearings. It was nearly impossible for him to step out of the house without a swarm of reporters or curious students dogging his footsteps. It was, in effect, house arrest and limbo.

"I'll try to write," Neill said rather grimly. "And it's not a good idea for you to go to court again, Joyce. They had you say your bit. As much as I want you there with me... Trouble spreads outward and right now I'm trouble."

"Not just now—always," Joyce corrected.

He was born for trouble; she was not. She thought her work was suffering at the clinic. Certainly, her emotions were in a constant state of turmoil and she wasn't any more sure of the outcome of this mess than he was.

The worst part for her was doubt. Despite his stirring speech, his protests of innocence, the lingering doubts were there, slivers she could not pull together. There was a secretive side to Neill and no one had scrutinized it more closely than Joyce had. How many times had he disappeared for a walk? How many times had she watched him, almost in mid-word, withdraw into his own world?

"Neill, would you tell *me* the truth?" Joyce asked slowly.

"I have. I will," he answered simply, "if I can."

"Did you have anything to do with the fund-raising for Ireland United?"

"No." He shook his head.

"But you are friendly with Michael Boyle and some of these others, friendly enough to know what they've been doing?"

He moved his head in a single nod.

"If you cooperated with the government..." Joyce began, but his warring look halted her. She was pleading their case, not his.

"Every man has to do what he thinks is right," Neill told her. "Even when I think a man is wrong or foolish, I tell that man but no one else. I'd fight that man in my own way but I'd never ask someone else to punish him for me. I can't say more about this, Joyce, not even to you."

"Did you have a hand in writing that dreadful *Catha* propaganda?" She hated herself for asking, but she wanted the whole truth and an end to doubt.

"You know the answer," Neill said bluntly. "You've been closer to me than anyone. Haven't you looked into my heart as well as my books and my brain?"

"I don't know. I really don't know." Joyce felt another chain, the cold chain of silence, being forged between them. "I believe in you, in your love and your work, but there's still so many things I don't know."

"I sign my name to everything I write. I'm no informer. Whatever it costs me—my passport or my soul—I won't do their job for them and I'll keep silent."

In a roundabout way he had just explained more than all the hours of testimony in court. Joyce surmised it was Michael Boyle who was responsible for *Catha,* but what she guessed at couldn't be testified to, and Neill adhered strictly to his own principles. Even when she didn't agree with him, she couldn't fault him. He was a man of honor and his word, in an era that found those ideas inconvenient and cumbersome. He was a nonconformist in some costly ways.

It wasn't an idyllic life by any means. People regularly appeared on the front steps and some of them were as motley a crew as Joyce had seen in any state hospital. They weren't dangerous or destructive, just weird.

Neill didn't notice or care. He'd met this one on a walk or that one in the park and offered his hospitality, his address, a meal or a bed for the night.

"Ireland is the land of a thousand welcomes, not Chicago," Joyce told him through clenched teeth. "Where did you find a retired rodeo rider? And why?"

"On Dearborn Street on my way to the lawyer," said Neill happily. "He and I fell to trading jokes in the elevator and when I figured out he was panhandling, I asked him to take a bite with us."

"You are a soft touch," moaned Joyce. She threw down her book and buried her face in a pillow. The old man was yodeling hideously or gargling in the bathroom. "Bag ladies, students of all shapes and sizes, a stray sailor, a coal miner and now, Buffalo Bill. Why?"

"For his story," hollered Neill as the volume of noise rose. "Poetry is the art of the glimpse, the distillation of a huge story down to a single drop of truth. I wanted to be the voice for those whose stories never got told."

"You are," she yelled back, "but it's his voice that's killing me. I had a tough day, Neill. I need some peace and quiet. He talks incessantly."

"I'll take him out for a walk and get you earplugs at the drugstore, if you like." He began to pace.

She nodded, content with any solution before there was permanent damage to her ears or their evening. "You'll wear out the carpet," she teased.

"How about your patience?" asked Neill.

"I'll let you know when to duck," Joyce promised him. "Tomorrow Julia and Frank want to drop by. I'm sure there's an ulterior motive when I haven't seen or heard from my family in so long."

"With such suspicion, you'd do well to apply for a job down at court." Neill broke off as their guest emerged, bellowing at the top of his lungs.

"Git along, little dogies/ It's your misfortune and none of my own," sang the old man.

Joyce flinched. Neill laughed.

Thankfully, there weren't many such visitors. The longer the hearings went on, the fewer people they saw. At first, his students came to visit in droves, but when Neill would not discuss what they wanted to hear, fewer stopped to chat. Even the faculty showing up thinned in number. Neill didn't care. He was as much an outsider in academic circles as anywhere else, and his tendency to poke fun at his stuffier colleagues hadn't endeared him to them.

Neill chafed a bit at the lack of company; he was used to working days and writing into the night, but there was little writing accomplished now.

His days were largely spent in courtrooms and law offices. He talked angrily to himself in the kitchen sanctuary, and he roamed from room to room in a parody of his usual wanderings.

Joyce thought of the caged golden-eyed panther in the Lincoln Park Zoo, his power confined and his natural instincts blunted. Neill, too, could survive without complete freedom and without room, but mere existence was not enough for inspiration.

So, the real nightmare stayed outside the house on Faculty Row, not inside. Joyce juggled her appointments at the clinic to rush downtown to the Federal Building. She heard angry, patriotic speeches from many of the defendants and the vicious whispers of the onlookers around her. She listened to descriptions of Neill as an undesirable alien, a rabble-rouser, and felt the sharp bite of her own nails in her palms.

He has the soul of a child, Joyce wanted to testify. He's impetuous and headstrong but that's no crime. He's easy to listen to and hard to understand, blunt and brutal in his poetry, but never cruel.

"Go home," Neill begged when he found her crying from frustration in the deserted corridor. "Better still, go away. Run away as far, as fast as you can."

"From you?" asked Joyce, raising her face to peer into the tortured depths of his eyes.

"I always did that. Ran to find a better place, ran to see a happier sight, ran to escape ugliness."

"From you?" repeated Joyce firmly, and he couldn't force himself to say the words to send her packing.

"Holy cow," said Julia. She walked past Neill and Joyce, went through the first floor of the house, and back to them. With her rounded belly and wide eyes she looked like an exploring raccoon. "What happened? Half an earthquake?"

Frank said nothing, as usual. He took the cup of tea Joyce offered him and turned on the television to sneer at *Meet the Press*.

"Welcome to Compromise City," explained Joyce. "The dining room is all mine. The kitchen is Neill's. We had to split this room in half. Don't sit over there near any of Neill's junk, by the way. If you lose his place in a book, he will kill you."

"By the death of a thousand paper cuts," Neill agreed solemnly. "If you move a scrap of paper with my writing on it, something far worse happens."

Julia shifted her eyes nervously back and forth. "What?" she asked finally, settling gingerly on the cleared half of the couch.

"He loses his temper and shouts," said Joyce, and she and Neill started to laugh in concert.

"Shut up, you morons," growled Frank at either the video images or Joyce and Neill. The panelists kept arguing and the couple kept laughing, unperturbed.

"You'll have to excuse us," Neill wheezed. "We don't get many visitors anymore. I didn't have many social graces to begin with, and Joyce has forgotten hers."

"No need for them," snorted Joyce. "Go look upstairs if you like, Julia. The bathroom's a free-fire zone, the bedroom is no-man's-land. I'm sure Mother wanted a full report."

"How did you...?" Julia had the good taste to get flustered, but she also headed immediately for the stairs. Out of earshot, she attempted a few lame excuses as to why she and Frank had stayed away this long and why the Laniers were very concerned about Joyce.

"I'm not having a nervous breakdown or being held prisoner. You can set their minds at rest." Joyce held up a blue-blotched brassiere and sighed. "Neill's week for laundry. He sorts by size, not color."

"This arrangement isn't going to work," Julia snapped peevishly. "This isn't like you."

"It is. It's just like me," argued Joyce. "You're the slob and Frank is neat. How do you handle the problem?"

"We fight." Julia surveyed the closet with Joyce's clothes and the two chairs strewn with Neill's division of his clean and dirty clothes.

"We don't," said Joyce. "I'll fight when I think Neill could change his habits, but he's as set in his ways as I am. I'll fight if it's life-or-death but not for blue laundry."

Her sister groaned. "A string divider across the living room? Give me a break. This is an armed truce. If anybody should know, it's me. Admit it's rotten and go back to the apartment."

"You can't go home again," Joyce quoted with a grin. "Actually, I'm very happy living in the pressure cooker. The heat's all outside, but we're cozy in here."

"Calm before the storm," was Julia's judgment as they rejoined the men. Her mission accomplished, she nagged at Frank until he relented and agreed to leave before he'd won his point with the TV announcer or the chess game with Neill.

"I thought we were too much like them," Joyce said. She went to her end of the couch and stretched her legs out to twine with Neill's somewhere in the middle. She rubbed her bare instep along his calf and made a contented sound.

"Like *them*? God forbid," moaned Neill. He crumpled up the sheet of foolscap in his hand and threw it back over his side to join a hundred other wadded balls littering the floor. "They loved each other for a weakness, not a strength. Your sister uses her feelings like knives on him. Frank uses his silence like a wall to keep her at bay. We love each other out of strength."

He bent his head for a moment and scribbled a few words, sneered at them and they, too, were discarded. Joyce watched the process, so familiar by now and still fascinating. The size of the yellow paper dune told her his writing wasn't going well. Every few days he ceremonially swept up and burned the evidence of his frustration. The papers were back, thicker than ever, in no time, but Neill persisted.

"They strike sparks off each other," Joyce said softly. If he wasn't listening, it didn't matter. She needed to say it aloud. "So do we, Neill. Sparks of anger and passion and jealousy and pleasure, and they call it love. So do we, but it's different. I can feel it now, but I don't know how to explain it."

She ducked, but not soon enough. The wad of paper bounced off her cheek and rolled down her chest. Neill caught hold of her ankle and tugged her down before she grabbed the handiest weapon, a lace-edged pillow, to retaliate.

"I wanted peace," he growled, biting playfully at her toes. "Did you hear that, woman? Peace in my soul. Peace in the wild kingdom of my brain and—" his white teeth nibbled at her heel until she squirmed and writhed "—peace for my body at night."

Joyce laughed and tugged but she succeeded only in flinging most of herself off the cushions and onto the carpet. Her foot was still his prisoner and Neill was doggedly working his way up to her knee. She was helpless with silliness and tears.

"I needed your quiet self and loved you," Neill grumbled, sliding off his perch to pin her down. "But have I got it? No, you rowdy, bothersome creature. You won't let me be at peace."

"This is the eye of a hurricane," Joyce said, smiling happily up at him. "The storm's out there, Neill, and this is as peaceful as it gets."

His leg moved purposefully between hers even as Joyce's fingers were busy with the buttons on his shirt. They would wrestle, but it wasn't going to be a fight, and they both knew there wasn't going to be a loser.

"Then it'll have to do," said Neill. His face hovered over hers and he mouthed three other words.

She couldn't hear them enough. She wouldn't tire of them, no matter how many times he said "I love you," no matter how many ways he showed her.

Through the windows of the courtroom, she watched the season change. There were a lot of indictments to hear, to return or dismiss. The winds picked up, sending a few leaves fluttering by and the publicity was dying down now that the end was in sight.

The day the grand jury assembled was the essence of autumn. Everything seemed cooler, slower—even the monotone of the voice reading the findings. The list was alphabetical. Joyce wiped damp palms on her skirt and heard Michael Boyle, Costello, Donnelly, Fitzgerald handed over for prosecution. She felt Neill's fingers seek hers. The droning voice went methodically down the pages. They did not look at each other, but his hand was cool, hers was on fire. "Malone...Mayhew..."

Neill's case was dismissed for insufficient evidence. In bland, flat words, the clerk delivered the end of a nightmare and the beginning of Neill's freedom.

"It's over!" Joyce exulted as the courtroom was being cleared, and she squeezed Neill's hand. She felt giddy, drunk, silly with the realization. "Finally, over!"

His fingers stayed curled around hers, engulfing her hand, and he raised it to his lips for a quick kiss.

"Thank God," Neill murmured. "Three months lost, twelve weeks of living in limbo, waiting for the ax to fall."

His arms fell to her waist. There was only time to share a long, deep look and a hug of victory before they had to face the press outside.

The questions were different now and the voices asking them were not quite as hostile or strident or demanding. Joyce kept telling herself this might be the last of the inquisitions. There were new scandals and trials and scoops to cover. It didn't make her dislike the circus atmosphere less.

Neill kept her close to his side as he muttered a few brusque answers and let out a little—very little—of the resentment built up throughout the proceedings.

"What's next?" urged one man, pushing a microphone into Neill's face. "Your job, Mr. Riordan?" "How's your book going?" shouted another.

"I'll be writing and teaching," Neill snarled. Joyce could feel the tensing of his arm and almost taste his longing to push the microphone into someone's ear. "I'll be doing what I'm supposed to be doing. What I should have done, in fact, if I hadn't been the unwilling, unwitting star of this poorly staged, badly written drama."

"Please don't be bitter," whispered Joyce.

She didn't want anything to mar this day or limit their celebration of the verdict. She didn't want to hang around the steps of the Federal Building one second more than necessary. Neill was starting to warm to the occasion; he couldn't resist the chance to pay back his journalistic tormentors a little.

"You've written reams all through this trial," Neill roared, "and most of it, bad prose. Yes, I have a book to finish and now, at last, my chance. Good riddance to all of you!"

"Temper, temper," Joyce cautioned, as Neill forged through the newsmen's gauntlet, shaking his head angrily at the rest of them. He must have heard her; he didn't respond to any more questions.

Once they broke free of their escort, Joyce had to stop herself from breaking into a run. The fall air was incredibly, deliciously cool. But she felt a summer's rush of heat and sunshine from inside her.

"I'm so happy," she told Neill. "I was getting scared that it would never end; it was going badly...a million depressing things."

"You? Scared? Depressed?" Neill looked astounded. "It didn't show, love. I've been the long-faced one, the sad, caged animal. I kept going the last few sessions only by watching you, held up by you."

That did it. The tears she had held back so long came. There was no warning or welling up. She buried them too deeply, along with her doubts, and the tears erupted. She wept all the way back to Neill's, letting the conflicting emotions wash away. Her worry and tension were too closely mixed with relief and happiness to separate.

"There should be champagne," Joyce suggested when she finally brought the sobbing under control. Neill was silent, stroking her back in an embarrassed, helpless way. "Okay, I'll split a beer for a toast but you have to get it."

She sat on the couch and contemplated the empty street through the open curtains. An empty street, a quiet house and a mute Neill was not what she'd expected. Today called for a party, jubilation, making love, dancing all night.

Neill came back from the kitchen with one glass and the bottle. "I have something to say," he said before he gave her the glass, "and it won't go down well, whether it's with beer or champagne."

"Go ahead," Joyce urged, still a little hoarse from her outburst.

"I need time alone," Neill began slowly. "I don't want you to leave, but I think there's no other way for us. We're both exhausted and worn thin by what's happened. I haven't put two words together on paper in weeks and I haven't been able to think beyond each day, but now I have to."

She wasn't sure she heard him right, but Neill looked so uneasy and uncomfortable, his posture was eloquent enough. "You finally managed to say it. Go. You want me to go."

"No, not want. I *need*...I need a few days alone, and a few weeks to sort out what's past and what's ahead," Neill protested loudly. "Trust me."

He took a step forward, gesturing at Joyce with the glass in his hand, but all she saw was a red haze of anger and blinding confusion. She was on her feet, too drained for more tears and too hurt for words. With a single flick of her wrist, her glass went spinning across the room, shattering on the end table.

"That's a change," she managed to eke out. "You've always been a man for now—just now—as if tomorrow didn't exist." There weren't many tomorrows to begin with. She didn't expect to hear there were none left.

He tried to grab her, but her quickness in evading him was born in the fury growing in her. Joyce had never imagined the pain of such rejection, only the pain of losing Neill when this year ended.

"Calm down and be reasonable," Neill urged. It sounded like one of her lines, and Joyce laughed coldly. "Let's talk."

"You've won. I'm going," she spat at him over her shoulder. "What else could we possibly have to discuss? The rent I owe you for three months?"

Charging up the stairs, Joyce heard the beer bottle meet the same fate as her glass. Neill's voice followed her even if he didn't.

"Half of Shakespeare's plays weren't even published before he was dead. Do you want the same fate for me?" There was a plaintive tone she hadn't heard often in his call. "My book's been on hold too long, Joyce."

"So have I," she screamed back down. A good scream relieved as much frustration as her tears had. "On hold, on standby and this affair was a one-way ticket from the start."

Neill's feet thundered upstairs and Joyce slammed the bedroom door shut. It was the last trace of prudence, she decided, and it was not to prevent him from violence. It was to prevent her from beaning him with anything heavy.

"Joyce, love, this is proof positive we need a break, both of us," cajoled Neill with such sweetness that ordinarily she would have melted. "It won't be long, darling. Open the door and we'll thrash it out."

"I'll thrash it out of you," Joyce mumbled, pulling her clothes out of drawers and closets. For good measure, she left the debris of hurry scattered all over. This was how she'd first seen his house; this was how she'd leave it. "Shut up, Neill."

"There's so much to do." He hammered on the door. "I've got such a little time left to do it in." The doorknob twisted back and forth and the wood creaked as if he were going to break it down.

Nimbly, Joyce stuff the suitcase full, pushed it off the bed and kicked it over to the door which she flung open. Neill shot through, propelled by his own force, and howled when his shin connected with the suitcase's hard edge.

"I'll get my other stuff later—at your convenience, of course," she said snidely while Neill limped after her at a safe distance. "I should have known...I should have guessed this was coming after that touching speech about holding you up, getting you through. I can't write the poems, however, so..."

Neill stopped saying, "Listen to Me," and lost the veneer of control. "You don't understand, dammit. You don't know everything and, seemingly, you've forgotten how to listen. I'm not letting you down easy...."

"Boy, you can say that again. You don't pull your punches with anyone—man, woman or child. And your sense of timing is unbelievable! The frost is on the pumpkin, Neill. You have, what? About eight weeks more and you're off the hook. You'll be back on the yellow brick road, chasing after whatever it is you're after."

She kicked the suitcase off the top step and let it bounce all the way down the stairs. The more she raged, the calmer Neill became.

"You're doing a better imitation of a Riordan tantrum than anyone I've ever seen," he said.

"I've heard you rant in the courtroom and rave in the kitchen for twelve weeks," retorted Joyce. "I stood by and watched you act looney tunes. The crisis is over and so are we, I understand that. You were selfish, obsessive..."

She recalled her earlier cry of triumph. *It's over.* She didn't know she had the terrible gift of prophecy.

Neill leaped ahead of her and barred the front door with his body. He didn't sound angry but hurt, even desperate. "I'm all those things and perhaps worse. But I've always lived and worked alone before and so have you! I know what it cost me to get through the trial. I can only guess what toll it took of you, how difficult I was to put up with. You were what I needed and you were here!"

"But now I'm intrusive? Upsetting?" Joyce wanted to hit him, but there was also the faint stirring that always came when they stood so close. She could resist it and after a while it would die without Neill to refuel the fire he'd set in her. And he was sending her away. "Too much of a good thing," she added cruelly to keep her tears in check. "Too much heat not to burn out. It's over."

"Not quite," Neill said. He started to reach for her and she struck out at him with the hair dryer. He pulled back, defeated by her anger. "I love you, Joyce, but the words alone aren't any good if you no longer believe them. We need a breather, both of us. The words weren't even the truth until you believed them, were they?"

She glared at him until he stepped aside. Her body brushed his in the only farewell she would give him and her hand pushed his from the suitcase handle. "I can manage nicely by myself," Joyce hissed, although she felt anything but nice.

"I'm not so sure about that," Neill yelled at her back. "For either of us. But we'll see. And I'll see you." Each phrase was louder and louder as she retreated down to her car.

As Joyce drove away, Neill was left standing on the porch shouting. She rolled up the windows, blasted the radio at full volume and she could have sworn she could still hear her own name echoing in her ears. Every time her heart bumped painfully in her chest, its beat was the short, anguished sound of Neill's voice calling her name. But she hadn't abandoned him; he had deserted her.

Everything else changed in one short year—less than a year—knowing Neill. Now her own name was going to haunt her because it happened to be a famous Irish writer's name and she could still hear Neill saying it. He could make it a caress, a threat, a whisper, a sob. She spent her first night alone in three months both crying and picking out a new name for herself. There wasn't one that captured her unhappiness.

Eleven

There was no going back. By morning Joyce had analyzed the situation and realized her pride had suffered most. Their affair was destined to end, sooner or later. She hadn't expected it sooner and her uncharacteristic outburst had been the result. Yesterday was as dark as the sunglasses she wore to hide the circles under her eyes.

There was no looking forward. Even if Neill called and pleaded with her to move back in, she knew the answer. Living in a pressure cooker once was plenty. She was back on the shelf she designed for herself, safe and secure, always knowing what came next. She'd met a once-in-a-lifetime man and known a once-in-a-lifetime love.

But Neill did not call. So much for protestations of unflagging love, she thought. The days dragged by and her pride did not quite fill up the emptiness of the nights. She brought out old lists of projects, reminders of how organized and planned she used to be, and did them all, but after each one was finished, it felt more like an exercise than an achievement.

"We have a new recruit for the space patrol," Margaret diagnosed one morning.

Joyce looked toward the child who was having a shouting match with her parents. "Cindy's no newcomer. You must be losing it, Margaret. She's an old hand here."

"I was referring to you," her secretary said dryly. "You should see yourself. You don't smile, you jump when the phone rings, and you've gone...lackluster. That's it! Tell Dr. Kyler you've got more kids than anyone else on staff and give up the parent group. Take a vacation!"

"That's what I'm on, a vacation," Joyce said cryptically. She corralled the "mouth" who was offering encouragement to Cindy, made peace all around and quick-stepped him into her sanctuary.

What was clear to Margaret was obvious to Joyce herself. Leave of absence from Neill was a breather but the air no longer crackled with excitement and wasn't as rich to breathe. Wearing the brightest colors didn't relieve the drabness of life without him. Giving a diamond sparkle was no gift when there wasn't Neill to shine for. Giving her a taste for adventure wasn't much help when her treasure hunt now was through junk stores for a cradle to refinish.

There was no remedy but time. It had been scary to live so intensely but the time had flown. In the midst of a situation she had every control over, days had been minutes when Neill was with her. There was nothing boring or humdrum for three months in Neill's house. Now the weeks piled up in the gentle, unchanging routine of her life. Two, three, four weeks and no Neill.

There were only familiar faces to see; with Neill, she encountered more strangers than a delegate to the U.N. There was only the placid, even road to follow again. Neill had pushed her to cope with emotions and needs she'd never felt so keenly. It had been scary, but it had also been exciting.

A package was delivered at her apartment. Joyce took one look at the foreign stamps, harps and queens, and set it down, unopened, on her drum table as if it was a letter bomb. There was only one person who would send her a gift from Ireland, and he wasn't even supposed to be there yet.

She put on her heavy yellow rubber gloves again and went back to stripping the carved walnut cradle for Julia. Her eyes were watering from the strong fumes, of course. It was the painstaking effort of following the intricate detailing and scraping out the wrinkled bits of paint that made her hands cramp and shake, not nerves. In less than ten minutes her curiosity proved stronger than her pride.

Joyce brought the carton into the kitchen and sat crosslegged on the canvas tarp she was working on. The cradle swung very slightly, as if it were already filled, reminding her how soon it had to be completed. She was careful not to spoil the stamps; one of her patients was an avid philatelist.

The customs declaration was no poem but it was as poignant and spare as some of Neill's efforts. *Gifts, glass, fragile,* someone else's handwriting proclaimed. Her heart? She didn't want a farewell gift and she would never need a reminder of Neill Riordan.

If they weren't so beautiful, she would have broken them. Instead, Joyce held the tall, faceted glasses up to the light, one in each hand, and saw their rainbow flashes reflected on the walls and spill across the floor. There was no champagne in the refrigerator, no toast to make and no one to drink it with in sparkling Irish crystal.

Not a word. Not a phone call. She was alone in the same city with a man who swore she was the only one whose opinions counted with him, a constant star he relied on for light to see his way. But Neill had said countless extravagant things before, and she had believed him when they were together.

There was no one to vent her feelings on.

Joyce cursed Freud and his stupid growth-from-separation theory, but she put the glasses away as carefully as crown jewels. They could gather dust, hidden and unused in the back of a cabinet, because they were meant to be brought out only for one man. And Neill knew another man's mouth would never rest on the rim, curve in a secret smile and whisper one of the silly, lovely things he told her.

He sent not a word or a phone call but a message she could shatter or save. Neill knew her. He knew her better, deeper and more intimately than any other person on earth. She saved beauty, not destroyed it. She saw the symbol of the two glasses, not one, empty but waiting to be filled. They were separate but not alone. She knew him, too. Wherever he was, Joyce was still with him and she would be again. She had a promise as fragile as glass.

The phone rang once and Joyce grabbed it before the second ring, knowing she was a fool.

"I'm coming over." Julia hung up before Joyce said no.

The announcement on the phone was predictable. Julia and Frank were locking horns over the Lamaze classes. The father-to-be claimed that anything billed as natural childbirth, by definition, didn't require lessons, turning in his stopwatch. Julia was adamant that Frank would not be deprived of the most meaningful moment in human history, even if he had to be gagged and dragged into her delivery room. Joyce suggested compromise after compromise and managed to make both of them so furious with her, they had actually united temporarily and stopped visiting her.

The incident enlightened Joyce. Not the couple's fighting, of course, but her ability to finally step away and see what was at the heart of their discord. Frank wasn't any more opposed to the classes than Julia was. It was because Julia insisted he do something she wanted; it was a silly version of "you can't make me," a power play where neither of them needed to use power, but love.

The shrill phone rang again and Joyce let it. It was a waste of breath to tell Julia she wasn't going to be the referee in any more domestic quarrels. It would be depressing for her to reveal to Julia that none of her own problems with Neill had been over power. There hadn't been a boss. Neill was gone. Julia and Frank were still setting off fireworks and firecrackers in each other. The phone persisted.

"Kill the fatted calf. I'm coming over."

The same words sounded very different when Neill was saying them. There was jubilance in his voice and, despite every cell and fiber flashing, a caution to her. She wanted to shout yes, yes, yes. To see him! To hold him!

To say good-bye.

Joyce was too excited and confused to force out an answer. Only after Neill asked her if she was there a few times could Joyce say she was with any surety.

"Yes, of course. Where are you? Dublin, Belfast, Galway?"

"I'm at the Billy Goat's phone booth with a handful of change, an armful of gifts and a mouthful of grand announcement. I can be there in half an hour, the Chicago Transit Authority willing."

He'd been here for the entire month without bothering to call her once. Suddenly, he wanted to be with her ten minutes before he called. Joyce bit her thumb.

A month alone had purged most of her anger and her pain. The residue was sadness for what had been and was no more. Without the taint of one unresolved argument,

Joyce could hold the memories of Neill like a treasured keepsake in her heart. They had shared so much and more intensely than most. The good, the fun and laughter of this year far outweighed the tears she'd shed.

If she saw him once more, she could let go of whatever bad feelings remained. She could say what needed saying and say good-bye.

"A half hour's not enough. Whatever's waited a month can wait a little longer, Neill. Make it about seven o'clock?"

It was a risk, of course, but the final one Joyce would take. As she paced the apartment, she weighed the factors carefully. To see Neill and clear the air was mature and responsible; it was better to part as friends. Then, nothing would take him entirely away from her.

Blissfully anonymous, self-sufficient once more, Joyce was her own woman. The danger in seeing Neill was that she would remember when she was also his woman. There were plenty of men who could make life hell but only one who could make it heaven.

As she was getting dressed, Joyce thought about the first dinner she'd made for Neill. Valentine's Day and February were a century ago. This night would be their last together, but a celebration of sorts was overdue. Her reflection in the mirror showed only how good the long, knife-pleated plaid skirt and white silk blouse looked, not how she felt. She moved closer to the cheval mirror to put another coat of brown on her pale lashes. The mascara was waterproof; it didn't matter if Neill's "grand announcement" made her cry tonight. There were a few parting shots she wanted to deliver, no matter what, and one last kiss.

She wouldn't break down or do a Julia scene. The news most likely was his decision where he was going next. Now that the furor of publicity had died down, Neill was free again in every way. He could pick and choose his next position; he could follow the lure of the next place. The notoriety only added to his legend, in the long run. *The next love?* Joyce bit the inside of her cheek and turned resolutely away from her own image. That thought produced pain and the pain showed too clearly in her face. She loved, not wisely, but too well.

She could lecture herself, reasonably and rationally, that she had no right to be this unhappy. This had been her year of the poet, her decision, and there would never be another one like it. She had not lost anything this year but her heart. *And you gave that gladly,* she thought.

The doorbell made her jump and realize how anxious she was. It was too soon to be Neill, she noted as she checked her watch. Prayerfully, it was not Julia with her predictable problems and the need of a sympathetic ear.

"I'm early," Neill said. "I couldn't wait another minute, so I persuaded a kind soul to give me a lift." He almost bowled Joyce over in his haste to get in the apartment and deposit a bottle of champagne and briefcase on the table. Unencumbered, he grabbed Joyce tightly and swung her around in a short, dizzying whirl, kissing her and laughing in alternate bursts. "I was skulking in your lobby, trying to make a dignified and punctual appearance."

Whatever his news was, his smile was triumphant and his mood was contagious. Joyce was afraid she'd get the nervous giggles and ordered him to put her down. "This must be big stuff. I haven't noticed you worried about appearances or punctuality before."

Neill put her at arm's length and gave her an appreciative look. "Well, I don't care about such things, but you do. You got all dressed up with no place to go, didn't you? That's very elegant on you, but it's no match for you in your green bathrobe." He unbuttoned the top two buttons on her blouse and put his mouth lightly on the white triangle of skin revealed there.

"Thank you...I guess," Joyce said uneasily, pulling back. "Neill, don't do that!"

She braced herself to look back at him, really look at him. Rumpled, disheveled and wearing the ugliest of his baggy jackets, Neill was still handsome. A few pounds lighter, she judged quickly, and he didn't appear any more rested than he had a month ago. And he was hairy!

"Oh, that beard and mustache!" she exclaimed. Against her better judgment, she laughed. She was supposed to be the old calm, cool, collected Joyce, not a simpering admirer. "Ugh!"

Neill smiled, oblivious to her comment, and briskly rubbed the thick reddish growth covering his big jaw and his upper lip. "I didn't see a need to shave since you left, so I didn't. Devilishly distinguished, aren't I? Sort of a Finn mac Cumhail image, I think."

Joyce snorted helplessly behind her hand. "I don't quite see you as the legendary Irish hero, Neill. It may be that ghastly tweed but you look more like Redbeard."

"The pirate?" He seemed delighted and struck an appropriate pose.

"No, Redbeard the wino," she said, and turned away to cackle to herself.

"I missed you." He stretched his hand out and it grazed her waist. She took another step. "Like a man who loses a leg and still has the phantom feeling. You were there but not there."

She would not relent and allow him to hold her. It would be impossible to let him go. "You knew exactly where I was. I can't say the same for you."

When she turned back, Neill frowned. "This is a night for celebration. Don't you dare put those pale, sad eyes on me," Neill warned softly. "You cry and I melt, as you well know."

"I'm not crying," Joyce denied hotly. The tears were all inside, clogging her throat, making it hard to breathe. It was unfair to be asked to celebrate his good-bye along with his freedom. "I'm confused, Neill. No, I'm upset...and confused. We got through a perfectly miserable couple of months together in great shape. You came out of it free as a bird and sent me off on my own again. Now, because you say so, it's a celebration. Better late than never, eh?"

"Are you trying to pick a fight?" Neill grabbed her hand as she spun around and jerked Joyce to him.

"Maybe," Joyce said belligerently. "It will make our ending more final if I'm good and angry when you leave tonight. But I don't want to fight with you. I was planning to be my usual amiable self."

She gave him a solid thump in the chest and pushed him away. What had worked on a fat precinct captain didn't budget Neill. He smiled and let her go. She took the crystal glasses out of the cupboard and brought them out to him.

"They're lovely. Let's drink a toast to your news and old times and call it a night." So much for her maturity, she thought. Ten minutes and the sparks were flying.

Neill peeled the foil from the bottle and sent the cork ricocheting off her wall. His voice rolled out at her, smooth and sure. "I wasn't planning on leaving tonight. I was thinking in terms of a very long evening."

He poured the straw-colored wine and the glasses sat there, untouched. The streams of bubbles rose and burst at the surface the way of Joyce's good intentions. "A toast to your dinner and my news. Or shall we skip over all and go right to the dessert?"

"Only if it's just dessert," Joyce said snidely. "I didn't make dinner."

"It doesn't matter. It's you I'm starving for." The gray eyes took on a silver glint she knew very well."

"Don't you dare give me that look," Joyce said. She narrowed her own eyes and let the muscles of her face freeze into a cold mask. "You can charm the grand jury or a snake out of a basket but it didn't always work on me. You managed to do without me these past weeks, haven't you?"

"Not very well," Neill said so quietly she almost missed his words. "But, of course, I had to make do with what I had." He went abruptly and grabbed the briefcase. "Here," he said, jamming it into her hands. "See for yourself. The work speaks for itself, as I'm fond of saying, and this work is you."

Joyce sat heavily on the couch and fumbled with the clasp. The sheaf of papers inside was typed, ordered and numbered. She knew before she read the title page she was holding his third book, finished against all odds after two years and this chaotic, crazy experience.

"Oh, it's done," she said in a small, disbelieving way. "How—how could you possibly think...or..." Her eyes grew moist, filling with a wondrous admiration, making reading it impossible. "This does call for a celebration!"

"Don't do that," Neill begged. "I had to do it and have it done before this year was out. It's for you but I knew if you were with me too much, I'd be too distracted to finish the race against time. Writing is a solitary trade and I've spent too long in that ugly, lonely house keeping bad company. Myself."

She didn't know what to say. Her fingers ran over the title, *Daughter of Lir*, as if she were reading braille, while a few traitorous tears fell on the paper. Turning the page quickly to hide the evidence of her feelings, Joyce stopped and read, through the blur, the table of contents.

There was nothing wrong with her memory, but there were no titles she recognized from his reading of works-in-progress. *Too bright, her face?* That one didn't sound like anything Neill Riordan wrote. She opened to a page at random and read.

The poems were more than for her. Most of them were about her. Her head swam in Neill's sea of erotic images and the rush of her blood filled her with heated energy. How could he put into such bold, beautiful words what was so intensely and privately shared between them?

"It's—it's—" Joyce began, and realized she was stammering. She settled for looking at Neill in quiet amazement.

"Not my usual stuff, eh?" Neill stood wide-legged in front of her and tipped her chin back until she was forced to meet his searching gaze. "Well, I haven't been my usual self since I met you. I worked on them all these months and couldn't manage to do one that didn't touch on us in some way or other."

"Touch is an understatement," gulped Joyce. "Neill, the one I read was a marvel but it was rather...well, rather *explicit*."

"Yes," Neill said with a little grin. "I'm not a terribly subtle fellow, am I?" He bent down and kissed her nose. "Devious, sullen, forgetful, irresponsible, but not subtle. You'll have to sue me to stop publication, you know."

The mere thought of publication and of how many people would read these poems was enough to render her speechless for a minute. Then, her normal, sensible brain started to work again. "You're kidding," Joyce said with a puckish smile. "No one will have a clue as to who Lir's daughter was. There isn't a mention of my name, and no dedication."

"They'll know," said Neill with authority. He pulled the manuscript away and dropped it on the red velvet next to her, pulling her to her feet. "Everyone will know. You'll have to get used to some sly, sidelong stares, I'm afraid."

"No one will know unless you tell them. Please don't," Joyce pleaded. "It won't serve any purpose. You'll be long gone by the time the book is published. I'll be part of your history and that's a far cry from being part of literary gossip. I don't want to be famous."

"You still don't get it, do you?" Neill ran his fingers through his hair and made it stick up wildly, the fox brush that would not be tamed. "Joyce, I love you."

She believed those three words as she had never believed in anything else. Her love for him had fed withered roots in Neill if he could talk about a home and children. His love for her produced a book of beauty, but he would never be caged, held by anyone.

"I love you, too," she whispered, dropping her head.

"And you need me."

"I do not," Joyce argued, without conviction. "How do you figure that? I don't *need* anyone." Be free, be who you have to be, she thought resolutely.

"You do," said Neill obstinately. "You need a little friction and that's me, the abrasive factor, in your life. How else does a diamond shine when there's nothing else hard enough to polish it?"

"You certainly have the rough edges," admitted Joyce. "It would take a sledge hammer to knock some of them off."

"Just a kiss," Neill said. "Just a home." He glanced over at the cradle in the corner. "And before I get too old to fly kites with them, a few more Riordans. This isn't, by chance, a poetic way of making your own grand announcement."

"I don't take chances," Joyce reminded him. "I never have."

"Oh, yes, you do," Neill said tenderly. "You took chances with me no other woman would. You trusted me. You stood by me and kept me steady through it all. Take one more and say you need me with you, and I'll stay."

Joyce closed her eyes. "For how long? An evening...or eight weeks?"

"As long as you like."

"That's not funny," she said thickly. The glass she picked up sent out little whirling patterns of color as bright and ephemeral as hope itself. "No, I don't think that's a good idea. You need your freedom but I couldn't live that way. I won't exist day to day, moment to moment, always wondering what the hell is next. I'm a creature of habit and routine. I'm even in nature and temper; that's my strength."

"And I'm odd," he interrupted. "We're the universe when the odd and even are put together, aren't we? There's nothing else."

"There's nothing that's changed," Joyce said wistfully. "I'm not about to abandon my career to follow you with everything I own rolled up in a bundle. I'm not going to leave my family and friends and the places I feel rooted in to see if Zanzibar or Sydney or Tallahassee is better. It won't be right, not for either of us, and eventually, we'd fight and I'd leave."

"You'd be easy to find," Neill said. "But it won't be that way when we're married."

Joyce froze, unable to believe she'd heard him right. The heavy glass almost slipped from her fingers, but Neill was there to take it. He put it down and pinned her arms to her sides, resting their foreheads together.

"Marriage? With me here and you off, God knows where, teaching, writing and lecturing?" She'd never been good at following his strange logic, but it was impossible to comprehend this most amazing proposal of all.

"I won't be away very much. Oh, a seminar or a speech here and there. The poor misguided regents at the university want me to stay on. Fine, I said. Chicago is as good as any place."

"Marriage?" She heard herself repeating the word like a demented parrot. He was offering her a lifetime of coping with a moody, unpredictable man, years of living with strings dividing his rooms from hers, characters of all sorts traipsing in and out, and she could watch Neill struggle with his muse and his demons. She said it, not unkindly, but firmly, because that was the way it would be. "You've made me crazy, Neill," she finished softly, but her body sought his for a moment. He felt so solid and good after so long, she couldn't pull away.

"Fair enough. You've made me sane...well, saner," he replied implacably. "I've no house to rent after the year. The faculty gentleman on sabbatical will be back in January, but we can look around after we get back from Ireland."

"There you go again," muttered Joyce. She tried to ignore his fingers tugging her blouse out of the waistband. "That's dreaming, Neill. I haven't got a passport. I'm not going to the suburbs, much less Ireland or getting married. You don't want a house. You never have! Or a car or a permanent address or tenure..."

"I don't want a house, right. I want a home and I found one. There's no other place for me than in your arms. There's no home for me but you. Take me back in, cold-hearted and practical witch, and marry me."

She gaped at him, startled by his vehemence and the sudden foray of his hand to her breast. Neill gave her a grin, showing the funny, boyish gap in his teeth, and a very old, knowing look crept into his eyes.

"You can't even write with me around," Joyce said feebly.

"I couldn't have written *Daughter of Lir* without you," he countered. "And it's superb, I don't mind telling you."

"Modesty is not one of your problems." His fingers searched around and found their objective, eliciting an immodest response from a cresting nipple.

"December twenty-first," Neill whispered fervently into her ear before he nipped the pink lobe lightly. "It's the shortest day and the longest night of the year. What could be a better date to get married?"

"I don't know," Joyce said. She yelped when Neill applied a bearhug and shook her head at him. "No, I didn't mean I was agreeing to a date. Marriage is a serious commitment that requires thought and deliberation."

"You've had a whole year to think about it," Neill murmured. "You'll have forty years—fifty, God willing—to repent leisurely."

He snagged the champagne bottle without relinquishing his grip on her and motioned with his head toward the hallway and the bedroom. Some celebrations did not call for speeches.

There were a thousand other objections she could raise but one irrefutable fact. She loved him, unconditionally and forever. There were a thousand questions she wanted to ask, but fifty years was a long time.

Joyce put her arm around Neill's waist and indicated she could use a sip of wine. He raised the bottle to her lips and tipped it back too enthusiastically. When a few drops trickled from the corner of her lips, he laughed and, leaning over, licked them away.

"You see? It's settled. December twenty-first and Christmas Day. Two weddings for the price of one."

"What?" She sputtered.

He edged her a few steps backward, his hard thighs pressing against her soft ones. "We'll be married twice, of course. Once here for your people and once in Dublin, so my brothers and sisters and their lot can see it."

"Of course," Joyce said incredulously. "We wouldn't want to do anything the way normal, average, ordinary people do."

"No, we wouldn't," agreed Neill firmly. He hooked his leg behind hers and tipped her backward onto the couch. "I've wanted to see you naked on this red velvet monstrosity since the first night I visited. You can't imagine what a lovely image it produced in my mind—white, smooth skin on the soft, red plush. I take it you are willing?"

"To make love on my couch? Yes," Joyce said, even as his weight was settling on her.

"To marry me," Neill growled fiercely. He began to slip buttons through openings with amazing dexterity. "Say it."

"I need my head examined," whispered Joyce, "but yes. Or yes, yes, for two weddings."

"Everyone will know you are the daughter of Lir, then, won't they?" He couldn't resist teasing her, physically or verbally. He felt her squirm with embarrassment. "Won't they, Mrs. Riordan?" His lips traveled down her throat and farther, making her squirm with feelings much stronger than embarrassment. His hands moved up under the skirt, meeting no resistance.

"Yes." Her reply was muffled under the assault of his mouth, but Neill seemed satisfied.

It wasn't any use to attempt talking intelligibly for a while. A month of absence and yearning had left her feeling dull, colorless and hollow. Neill filled her, body, mind and spirit, and Joyce offered him the place he wanted in her arms and in her heart.

Dimly, she heard the urgent sounds and it was impossible to tell who made them. There was the hurry, the frenzy of both, the hoarse groans and the searching of eager hands. She hung, suspended in time and space, until Neill thrust himself deeply, heavily, into her and Joyce arched, lifted, to move with him. They were two separate people but formed one for the brief moments of total possession and complete union.

She understood the terrible tension and strain of his body, what he was reaching for with every stroke of his hips. Wrapped around him, she held Neill to the earth and he let her touch the sky, taking her far, far away with his love and his dreams.

He was lost in the rocketing pleasure that shook him. Joyce held him tighter, feeling her own shattering explosion slowly subsiding but unwilling to let go, unwilling to break the bond they formed. He looked down at her and Joyce smiled, reaching to caress his slightly rough cheek.

"Promise me that we'll never have another year like this one," she said. Her hands pulled his face to hers and her fingers ran through the beard, learning the new texture—not really soft, not quite rough. "Promise!"

Neill took the tip of her nose in his teeth and seemed to consider taking a bite of her. "Perish the thought. Some of them will be better. But, love, some of them will be..." He lost the thought on the way to her mouth.

For better or worse. It was a promise both of them would make and mean. The kiss she gave him meant he was the greatest adventure of all and the risks were worth it. Whatever was next, Neill would be sailing for the absolute limits of life itself and she would keep them both on course. Strong and steady, they were going together.

"Welcome home, darling," she whispered. "Welcome back."

WHAT LIES BEYOND PARADISE?

BARBARA COOPER

THEIRS WAS A DREAM THAT LED...

BEYOND PARADISE

atching the pulse of a
oman in the Twenties.
A woman with a dream.
man with all his dreams
attered. The search for a
ng-lost father. And the
scovery of love.
Available from 14th
arch 1986. Price £2.50.

ORLDWIDE

Silhouette Desire

COMING NEXT MONTH

LEADER OF THE PACK
Diana Stuart

Weylin Matthews made Jenna's dogs bark as though a wolf had walked into the camp. He seemed to have some mysterious power over her... When she looked into his eyes, she could refuse him nothing.

FALSE IMPRESSIONS
Ariel Berk

Brandon Fox didn't look like a typical girlie-joint customer — he was the handsomest man Audrey had ever seen — but he was there. And ogling was the word that certainly sprang to mind, since he couldn't seem to take his eyes off her. But first impressions are often false...

WINTER MEETING
Doreen Owens Malek

Leda knew Reardon was the one man she should avoid at all costs. But one glimpse of the pain and determination in his bleak gray eyes told her he was also the one man she could never turn away from.

Silhouette Desire

COMING NEXT MONTH

GOLDEN GODDESS
Stephanie James

What right did Jarrett have to demand her love? He was the wrong kind of man, with his fanatical interest in primitive art and antiquated ideas about women. But could Hannah be wrong, and Jarrett be Mr Right...?

RIVER OF DREAMS
Naomi Horton

Even as Leigh reveled in his arms she knew she couldn't afford the commitment he demanded. Soon she'd have to choose... before the perilous cruise had run its course.

TO HAVE IT ALL
Robin Elliot

Brant's reputation preceded him, and Jenna had her doubts about getting involved. He said he wanted them to have it all, but Jenna had more in mind than Oreo cookies and a pet Canary.

Rebecca had set herself on course for loneliness and despair. It took a plane crash and a struggle to survive in the wilds of the Canadian Northwest Territories to make her change – and to let her fall in love with the only other survivor, handsome Guy McLaren.

Arctic Rose is her story – and you can read it from the 14th February for just £2.25.

The story continues with Rebecca's sister, Tamara, available soon.

Silhouette Desire Romances

TAKE 4 THRILLING SILHOUETTE DESIRE ROMANCES ABSOLUTELY FREE

Experience all the excitement, passion and pure joy of love. Discover fascinating stories brought to you by Silhouette's top selling authors. At last an opportunity for you to become a regular reader of Silhouette Desire. You can enjoy 6 superb new titles every month from Silhouette Reader Service, with a whole range of special benefits, a free monthly Newsletter packed with recipes, competitions and exclusive book offers. Plus information on the top Silhouette authors, a monthly guide to the stars and extra bargain offers.

**An Introductory FREE GIFT for YOU.
Turn over the page for details.**

As a special introduction we will send you FOUR
specially selected Silhouette Desire romances
— yours to keep FREE — when you complete
and return this coupon to us.

At the same time, because we believe that you will be so thrilled
with these novels, we will reserve a subscription to Silhouette
Reader Service for you. Every month you will receive 6 of the very
latest novels by leading romantic fiction authors, delivered direct to
your door.

Postage and packing is always completely
free. There is no obligation or commitment —
you can cancel your subscription at any time.

It's so easy. Send no money now. Simply fill in and post
the coupon today to:-

SILHOUETTE READER SERVICE, FREEPOST,
P.O. Box 236 Croydon, SURREY CR9 9EL

Please note: READERS IN SOUTH AFRICA to write to:-
Silhouette, Postbag X3010 Randburg 2125 S. Africa

FREE BOOKS CERTIFICATE

**To: Silhouette Reader Service, FREEPOST, PO Box 236,
Croydon, Surrey CR9 9EL**

Please send me, Free and without obligation, four specially selected Silhouette Desire Romances and reserve a
Reader Service Subscription for me. If I decide to subscribe, I shall, from the beginning of the month following my
free parcel of books, receive six books each month for £5.94, post and packing free. If I decide not to subscribe I
shall write to you within 10 days. The free books are mine to keep in any case. I understand that I may cancel my
subscription at any time simply by writing to you. I am over 18 years of age.
Please write in BLOCK CAPITALS.

Name _____

Address _____

_____

_____ Postcode _____

SEND NO MONEY — TAKE NO RISKS
*Remember postcodes speed delivery. Offer applies in U.K. only
and is not valid to present subscribers. Silhouette reserve the right
to exercise discretion in granting membership. If price changes
are necessary you will be notified.*
Offer limited to one per household. Offer expires April 30th, 1986.

EP18SD